Catch Me
If You Can

Charles Ray

Uhuru Press
North Potomac, MD

This is a work of fiction. Characters, places, and events are the products of the author's imagination. Any resemblance to any character, living or dead, is coincidental and unintended.

The reproduction or distribution, by any means, including electronic distribution, is expressly prohibited without the written consent of the copyright holder, except for fair use quotes in connection with reviews.

For information about this and other works of this author, contact the author at charlesray.author@gmail.com.

Printed in the United States of America

Cover design by the author.

PROLOGUE

The full moon, like a tarnished silver plate, hung high in the obsidian blackness of the night sky, bathing the winding paths of the park in a bright glow, broken only by the inky shadows of the tall oaks, cedars, and maples that lined them.

But, he preferred the enfolding comfort of the shadows in the bushes that grew in profusion beside the paths, moving like a shadow himself, as quiet as a jungle cat in search of prey. And, in search of prey he was.

The park looked deserted this late at night, but he knew that if he looked long enough, that if he was patient, he would be rewarded. He lifted his left wrist and peered at the green numerals of the cheap watch he wore; 9:14; still early. The prey he sought would wait until closer to 10:00.

He knew this because he'd stalked this same area for nearly two weeks. He knew the trails his prey used, where they would stop. He'd seen them follow the same routine every other night for fourteen days like clockwork, and tonight was the night. He could feel his pulse pounding in anticipation. His patience would finally be rewarded.

So, he waited. He was good at waiting; standing for long periods of time, his only movement the turning of his head as he surveyed the scene before him or shifting his weight from one leg to leg to relieve the tension. He stood there in the darkness like one of the solid oaks and allowed the breeze off the nearby bay to slide across his skin.

Fortune smiled upon him.

They came from the western entrance to the park, the one not far from the main street that led downtown, just as he knew they would, just as they'd done every other night for the past two weeks.

The boy was tall and broad-shouldered, with his light brown hair cropped close to his bullet-shaped head, while the girl, her silvery-blonde hair handing just to her shoulders and framing a heart-shaped face, barely came up to his shoulders. The boy had his left arm draped over the girl's shapely shoulder, his hand cupping a generous breast that threatened to pop out of the flimsy bra that was clearly visible through the translucent, open-neck blouse she wore. She didn't seem to mind, the hunter noted, and was, in fact, rubbing her right hand across the bulging crotch of the boy's jeans.

"Animals," he muttered quietly. "Nothing but rutting animals. No sense of decency."

He felt the heat rising in his cheeks.

Half closing his eyes, he took slow, deep breaths to center himself. By the time the couple were passing the spot where he stood concealed in the shadows, he was again calm. He watched them through the narrow slits formed by his half-closed lids. Oblivious to everything but themselves they sauntered past, their hands now roaming over each other's bodies. Watching them, his lips curled downward in distaste.

Soon, you two will pay for your sins.

When they were well past him, and at a point where the path curved to the right, he began to move, staying in the shadows of the foliage he moved with the silence of a stalking jungle cat. He didn't need to see them.

They always went to the same spot. A clearing just off the path, a broad swath of grass near a great oak that they had, in the two weeks he'd been watching them, worn until the grass was now flat and withering. Not, he thought, that they would have noticed or cared.

By the time he arrived at a point in the bushes from which he had a clear view of the clearing, they had already partially undressed.

The girl lay on her back with her knees up, her skirt up around her waist, as the boy, his pants and undershorts removed and tossed casually in a messy heap, knelt at her feet, working her panties over her pale, fleshy thighs.

"Hurry up, Alan," the girl said breathlessly. "I got to be home before midnight."

"I'm goin' as fast as I can, babe," the boy said, straining to slide the flimsy garment over her lets. "Hold still, will you? Why'd you even have to wear drawers tonight? You knew we were plannin' to hook up."

"Aw, come on. A girl can't be going out without underwear. If my mom had noticed she'd have a fit."

The boy slapped her fleshy thigh playfully, eliciting giggles, then he set back to work dragging the flimsy garment down her wiggling legs.

An ordinary man would have, despite himself, been excited by what he was seeing, and might have even stopped to watch what was happening. But, he was no ordinary man. He was a man with a divine mission.

When the boy finally got the panties over her bare feet, he casually tossed them aside and began to position himself over her. The girl's eyes were closed and the boy was too preoccupied with what he was about to do, so, even if the man who glided toward them from the bushes had made noise it's unlikely they would have heard.

The first awareness of him was when he'd grabbed the front of the boy's head and pulled it back, exposing his neck and a bobbing Adam's apple.

"What the fu-" was all the boy could manage to say before the man's right hand swept around and made a slicing motion from left to right, slicing so deep that he severed both carotids, sending a geyser of dark blood spurting as if from a broken water main, splashing across the girl's face and naked breasts. The boy's hands released their grip on her shoulders and began to reach for the gash in his neck, but the strength, and the life, were leaving his body as rapidly as the blood that gushed from the gaping wound in his neck.

The girl's eyes flew open and were quickly filled with the thick blood gushing from above. She snapped them shut and opened her mouth to scream, but that orifice, too, received a splash of blood, causing her to make a gurgling sound.

The man grasped the dying boy by his right shoulder and shoved him aside, confident that the boy would be dead by the time his body hit the ground. He then knelt beside the girl who was wiping frantically at the blood that coated her face and chest.

"Those who sin must die," he said.

In her panicked state, the words were garbled, but she wiped at her eyes in an effort to get a look at the source of the disembodied voice. All she was able to make out at first was a dark figure looming over her. Then, a thin line seemed to be detaching itself from the figure, swinging up. At the end of the line, her blurred vision saw a glint of something that looked like the silver points they'd put on the stars for the junior prom the year before.

Then, the silvery thing was swooping down, down toward her. A part of her brain, at that last moment, realized what she was seeing and what was about to happen, and she opened her mouth to scream. But, her scream was cut off by a white-hot feeling in the

4

center of her chest, and suddenly, she couldn't breathe. Her chest felt like it was on fire. But, the feeling lasted for only an instant, to be replaced by a cold numbness that spread like water from an overflowing bathtub, from the center of her chest outward to every corner of her body. And then, there was nothing but blackness.

The man knelt there, smiling down at her as he watched, first the look of panic in her eyes as she realized what was happened, then the widening of those eyes in shock and pain as the nine-inch blade pierced her chest, slicing through her Aorta and Left Brachiocephalic Vein. Less than a heartbeat later, the light went out in her eyes. Her pupils dilated and her mouth went slack.

He let out the breath he'd been holding from the time he grabbed the boy. The hunt had been successful. But, he still had work to do. The scene must be just so.

He wiped the knife on the grass and returned it to the leather sheath strapped to his right ankle and set to work.

Charles Ray

CHAPTER 1

Detective Lieutenant Gregory Kildare sat at his desk, his size eleven shoes propped on an open drawer of his desk and flipped paper clips at the waste basket next to the radiator. He was bored and pissed in equal measure. Bored, because after three weeks into his new job as chief of detectives for the police department of Darden, a town of 6,500 people, mostly crab fishermen, on the western shore of the Chesapeake Bay, there'd been only one crime for his four-man detective section to investigate; a break-in and theft from Smedley's Hardware and Bait Shop on Main Street. The burglars had gained entry by breaking a window at the back of the store but had left nothing the forensics team could use to identify them. They'd also only taken a few low-value items, some fishing spears and a few knives that were popular with the local fishermen. They continued to investigate the case—mostly because James Smedley was the mayor's cousin and constantly harangued them to find the culprits and return his stolen merchandise, but it was going nowhere, and, Kildare thought, wasn't likely to ever be solved, unless the perps did something incredibly stupid, or talked to the wrong person.

He was pissed because he was pulling night shift, something he insisted he do along with his subordinates, and his partner, Detective Sergeant Larry Meade was an hour late—again.

Usually, always, in fact, on time for his day shift, Meade seemed to have problems reading a watch whenever his name was on the night duty roster. Not that there was much chance of anything coming up that would require a detective, but dammit, Gregory thought, protocol is protocol. You have duty, you do it.

He resolved to take a huge bite out of Meade's ass when he finally showed up.

In the meantime, he kept flipping paperclips at the waste basket, mentally cheering whenever one went in.

Just as his patience was about to reach its limit, and he was about to reach for the phone to call Meade and relieve some of his tension by yelling at him over the phone, the object of his anger came strolling through the door from the booking room, looking, as he always did, as if he'd stepped off the cover of *GQ*.

Broad shoulders tapered into a slender waist and thighs that were muscular without being gross, encased in a gray suit that had obviously been tailored to fit. His blond hair, which Greg knew didn't, as was the case with many men who had hair that color, didn't come from a bottle, and his oval face, with its patrician nose, was perpetually tanned despite the cloudy weather they'd been experiencing on the Chesapeake shores since Greg's arrival, but without the orange tint of someone who used a tanning bed. Greg couldn't help comparing himself to his partner. He was also broad shouldered, but at thirty-eight—four years older than Meade—was beginning to get a little pudgy in the middle, and his thigh muscles strained against his off-the-rock blue suit. He also had a perpetual tan, but as a result of his African and Native American ancestry rather than exposure to the sun.

As Meade approached his desk, which was jammed against Greg's so that they sat facing each other, Greg began forming in his mind what he'd say to his truant partner.

Before he could say a word, though, Meade walked to the side of his desk and smiled down at him, flashing his pearly white, perfect teeth.

"Sorry I'm late, partner," he said. "I had some family business to take care of, and it ran late."

Momentarily taken aback by the preemptive apology, Greg frowned up at him.

"You could've at least called to let me know you'd be late," he said.

Meade pulled his smart phone from his jacket and plugged it into the charger on his desk.

"I tried, but wouldn't you know it, I forgot to charge my phone yesterday, and the damn thing died on me. I didn't miss anything important, did I?"

Greg huffed. Had him there. The evening, so far, was about as boring as it could be. Even the uniformed officers he could see through the large window at the front of the office were standing around the booking room looking bored. He shook his head.

"Nah, you didn't miss anything. But, if the chief had been in, you might be in hot water for reporting late for shift."

"Aw, don't worry about Chief Hoag. Him and me go way back. He'd understand."

Greg didn't really need to be reminded that he was the outsider. Hell, David Hoag subtly reminded him at least once a day that he'd taken a chance on hiring an ex-DC homicide detective and put him in the senior detective slot over three men who'd been with the force since they got out of the police training school; not to mention several qualified men in the Anne Arundel County police or sheriff's office. It wasn't done in an unfriendly or threatening way, just the way people in South County, as they described themselves, talked.

He supposed if he stayed in Darden long enough, he'd get accustomed to the blunt way the watermen, which is what crab fishermen called themselves, talked. For now, though, it rankled. It rankled a lot.

He was just about to say something about it to Meade when Sandra Carter, the only black person beside him on the town police force, opened the door and leaned into the room.

"Hey, Kildare, Mead, you got a call. Two DBs in Raleigh Park," she said.

They looked at each other.

"She's pullin' my leg, right?" Meade said.

Greg shrugged.

"What's going on, Officer Carter?" he asked.

Carter, only half an inch over the minimum height requirement, who normally had a smile on her found face, looked harried.

"Hell if I know, lieutenant. Patrol officer just called in and said they found two dead bodies in the park and he needed detectives on the scene."

"That means the deaths look suspicious," Meade said.

Greg wanted to say he already knew that, but bit back the remark. If this *was* a homicide, he'd need to keep the relationship with his partner working well.

Damned if he was going to lose another one.

CHAPTER 2

Greg completed the police academy and joined the DC Metro Police Department as a patrol officer a week after his twenty-second birthday. He received his detective's shield just before his thirtieth birthday and after a year was assigned to the homicide division where, for seven years, he amassed a stellar record, with the highest rate of successful case closures than any other metro homicide detective, including the arrest of a K Street lobbyist who murdered his pregnant intern and dumped her body in Rock Creek Park. He'd become the detective with whom newly promoted detectives were partnered during their probationary period and was into the third week of his partnership with Antonio Nunez, a twenty-nine-year-old who had been a uniformed officer for six years.

He'd pegged Nunez as something of a loose cannon immediately and sought ways to temper his tempestuousness at every opportunity. Unfortunately, Nunez was also a hothead with zero sense of humor, and on the last morning of their partnership, Greg had innocently called him 'short round,' referring to his height, which was five inches shorter than Greg's five-eleven. Nunez, however, had taken the tag as a reference to his sexuality, and had been sulking all day, refusing to talk to Greg. He just sat at his desk, glaring down at the phone.

He finally looked up when the chief of detectives walked into the bullpen and directly to their facing desks.

"Okay, Kildare, I got a case for you two," he said. "There's been a jumper at the Crown Condo on New Hampshire Avenue. Get over there and get witness statements and make sure it is, in fact, a suicide, or accident. The dispatcher will give you the address on the way."

Greg stood and checked to make sure his service weapon, a Glock 19, was secure in his hip holster on his right side, and his badge was clipped to the left side of his belt. He noticed that Nunez, though still not making eye contact with him, did the same.

"You got it, chief," Greg said, and headed for the door.

They rode silently in the elevator to the basement which opened out into a parking lot behind the building and made their way to the white Ford Crown Victoria that had been assigned for their use. The only difference between it and the patrol officer vehicles was that it lacked the red and blue stripes and shield of the MDCPD and didn't have a light bar on the roof, but blue flashers mounted in the front grill instead.

Greg usually let Nunez drive, but thought he was being childish with the sulking and silent treatment, so, rather than tossing him the keys as he ordinarily would, he slid in behind the wheel and waited for Nunez to get in beside him and buckle himself in.

He keyed the radio and got the address on New Hampshire from the dispatcher as they were exiting the parking lot.

The drive from the precinct to the address was quiet, and icy, with Nunez sitting stiffly and staring out the windshield as Greg navigated DC's streets.

Thankfully, traffic was light, so he had no need to use their emergency lights or siren, and the voyage was mercifully short.

The CSI van and a technician from the ME's office had already arrived and the uniforms had yellow crime scene tape roping off the entrance to the building and a section of the sidewalk where Greg could see a large form in a black plastic body bag, and the edge of a dark red pool of congealing blood. A uniform stood on the entrance pad next to a tall blonde woman wearing a halter top that barely held her large breasts and shorts that Greg thought were cut way too high for her apparent age and the cellulite in her bulging thighs. She had a haunted look on her pale face, which was in sharp contrast to the red, freckled appearance of her upper arms, shoulders, neck and upper part of her chest, marking her as someone who spent too much time in the sun without a sunblock with a high enough sun protection factor for their light complexion.

He noted all this, and the fact that Nunez was still sulking, as he exited the car and strode toward the CSI tech who was standing over the others giving orders.

"Hey, Joe," he said. "Whadda ya got?"

Joe Simpson, a middle-aged white man with an expanding middle and a receding hairline, turned and smiled at Greg.

"Hey, Greg. How's it hanging? Allow me to introduce John Slater, male, Caucasian, 46-years old, and a resident of Takoma Park," he said. "Had a fatal collision with the sidewalk after coming off the fifth-floor balcony."

Greg's brows twitched. "You got all that from just lookin' at him?"

"Well, that and driver's license in his wallet that was in his pants pocket."

"His driver's license told you he jumped from the fifth floor?"

Simpson pointed at the blonde at the entrance. "Nah, got that from Adele Wilson over there. She occupies the fourth-floor apartment directly below where the vic fell from. She was sunbathin' on her balcony when he went flying, actually, fallin' past. Scared the shit out of her."

"Okay, Sherlock," Greg said. "You got a reason he'd jump?"

"Ah, now, that, my friend is where it gets interesting." He knelt and opened the body bag. "Take a look at this."

Greg had, during his time on the force, seen a lot of bodies, but kids and the victims of falls from high places still bothered him. He forced himself to look down. The left side of the victim's face was smashed and almost unrecognizable as human, while the right side was untouched. The head was canted at a strange angle. Must have landed face first, he thought.

"Okay, what am I lookin' at?"

Simpson opened the bag further and lifted the victim's right arm, pulling back a blood-stained shirt sleeve. "Look at the wrists," he said. "Notice the red markings, almost like something pressed real hard or gripped it."

Looking closely, Greg did notice the discoloration, about a quarter inch wide, encircling the dead man's wrist.

"Okay, I see it," he said. "What's it mean?"

"Well, if it was just this one wrist, I'd say nothing I could take into court. But, there are similar markings on the other wrist, and you'll see he has a bruise on his right cheek that's not consistent with injuries from the fall."

Slowly it dawned on Greg what the man was hinting at.

"You sayin' he didn't jump?"

Simpson snapped his fingers. "Give that man a cigar, folks. It might've been an accident, but my bet is someone was grappling with Mr. Slater. These bruises are all fresh."

Greg stood straighter and smoothed the wrinkles out of his trousers. He walked to the building entrance and stopped in front of the woman.

"You're Ms. Wilson, right?" he asked. "You called the police?"

The woman looked at him and blinked as if she'd just awoken from a deep sleep. Slowly, she nodded.

"Y-yes, I was the one who called 911."

Her lips trembled and her eyes darted from side to side.

"Can you tell me what happened, Ms. Wilson?" Greg asked in a soft voice. Out of the corner of his eye he noticed that Nunez was frowning at the woman.

She took a deep breath, shuddering as she exhaled.

"W-well, I was on my balcony . . . sunbathing," she said, biting her lower lip after every few words. "T-then, I heard these loud voices from above, in Mr. Lanham's unit, that's Daryl Lanham, he's the owner. Anyway, I heard this argument."

"What were they arguing about?" Nunez asked.

Greg shot him a harsh look, then turned back to Wilson, whose eyes had gone wide at Nunez's tone of voice.

"That's okay, Ms. Wilson," he said. "Take your time and tell us what happened."

"I couldn't make out what they were arguing about," she said. "I only heard a few words. I was standing just outside my door and the words were muffled by the ceiling, the floor for them, I suppose. Anyway, there was a scream, and I saw poor Mr. Slater falling past my balcony rail." She blinked back tears. "He was screaming and flailing his arms, and . . ." She shuddered and began crying.

Greg put a hand lightly on her shoulder. "Take a few deep breaths. You'll be okay. You knew the victim?"

"Y-yes," she said after gulping in a few mouths full of air and letting them out slowly. "He is, was, Mr. Lanham's brother-in-law. Mr. Lanham was married to his sister, but they got divorced about six months ago, but I guess they remained friends. A bunch of them always got together every Friday for a card game."

She'd calmed considerably once she started talking, but Greg had heard enough to know they no longer had a relatively simple case of suicide—simple in that he could pass it off to another team of detectives. This, though, was manslaughter or negligent homicide at a minimum, and he was pretty sure the chief would want him to stay on it.

"Okay, Ms. Wilson," he said. "I might have a few more questions for you later." He turned to Nunez. "Let's go up and see what Mr. Lanham has to say for himself."

Without responding, Nunez fell in behind Greg as he entered the building. He said nothing during the elevator ride to the fifth floor. Only when they exited the elevator and saw two uniformed cops standing with their backs to the wall, their eyes on a door down the corridor did he finally say something.

"What's going on here, guys?" he asked.

"Guy down there in the unit the vic fell from has the door barricaded," the nearest cop said.

"Did he say anything?" Greg asked.

"Yeah. Said if we didn't get away from the door, he was gonna kill the other two dudes in the place and then himself. We fell back here and called it in. S.W.A.T.'s on the way with a hostage negotiator. If the negotiator can't talk this guy out, they'll make entry from the apartment above. They told us to cover the door which is the only other exit from the apartment."

Greg nodded. It made sense to let the specialists in S.W.A.T. take care of what had become in effect a hostage situation.

He felt Nunez brush against him as he headed for the door.

"Tony, what the fuck do you think you're doin'?"

Nunez stopped and looked back at him, a sneer on his face.

"I never thought you'd be such a pussy, Greg," he said. "This is just a buncha old white guys. Dude's prob'ly bluffin'. Let's see who's a short round now, eh."

He whirled and kept walking toward the door.

"Tony, stop," Greg said in a harsh whisper. "You're violatin' procedure. We have to wait for the hostage team."

"Bullshit," Nunez said as he stopped in front of the door. "A waste of tax payer's money. I'll get these old farts out. You just watch."

He wrapped his fist on the door.

"DC Police," he said in the commanding voice they'd been taught in the academy. "Open the door and come out with your hands in the air."

"Go away," a muffled voice inside the condo said.

Nunez pounded on the door again.

"Last chance," he said. "Open the damn door, or I'll break it down."

What happened next would embed itself in Greg's conscience forever, causing him sometimes to wake up gasping for air.

There was a loud bang, and two overlapping, ragged holes appeared in the think wood of the door. Nunez bent at the waist, his hands going to his midsection. He took a step back and turned, and Greg saw that the front of his suit was shredded and beginning to darken with the blood pouring from dozens of dime-sized holes in his jacket.

He yanked his Glock from the holster and started forward, yelling at the nearest officer as he ran past him, "Call dispatch. Officer down. Shots fired." To the other officer, he said, "Cover me. I'm gonna try and get him away from that damn door."

As he neared his fallen partner, he noticed that the shotgun blast had mangled the lock, and the door was swinging inward. The gap between door and frame was just wide enough for him to see a slender, middle-aged white man breaking open a double-barreled shotgun. Torn between the need to neutralize a potentially deadly threat and aiding Nunez, he paused for a heartbeat. Self-preservation and years of training experience won out. He turned to the door and kicked it the rest of the way open and then went into a shooters crouch, his left side toward the man with the shotgun to present a smaller target, his Glock pointed at the man's chest in a two-handed grip.

"Drop the weapon and get down on the floor," he yelled.

The man looked up at him, his eyes maniacally wide. Then, he resumed trying to insert two more shells in the weapon.

Greg's actions were reflexive and instant. He took a deep breath, let it out, and squeezed the trigger three times. The Glock had very little kick as it popped three times, sounding like July Fourth firecrackers. The man stopped, a look of surprise on his face as three holes appeared in his chest in a tight group that a small hand could cover. Blood began to seep from the three wounds and soak the front of his shirt. Then, his eyes rolled up in their sockets, the shotgun and two shells fell from his limp fingers, and he dropped like a sack of wet rice.

Greg ran in and after kicking the shotgun away, scanned the room, noticing two other men, a light-brown-skinned man and a morbidly obese white man, crouched in the corner with their hands over their heads and expressions of absolute terror on their faces. He watched them out of the corner of his eye as he placed a finger on the shooter's neck, over the carotid. Feeling no pulse, He felt sure the man was dead. Just them, the uniformed cops came into the apartment, their weapons drawn.

"This one's dead," he said. "And, I assume the other two were the hostages. Take care of them, while I check on my partner."

"Ambulance is on the way," one cop said, as he walked toward the two crouching men, his weapon on them.

But, Greg wasn't listening. He ran back into the hallway, knelt and took Nunez's head in his hands. His partner's breath was ragged, and his eyes kept opening and closing.

"Hang in there, Tony," he said. "Help's on the way."

"G-guess you were right, Greg," Nunez said in a faint voice. "Shoulda waited for S.W.A.T."

"Damn, Tony, I'm sorry," Greg said. "I sometimes let my jokin' get out of hand. I didn't mean to insult you."

Nunez smiled weakly. "That's okay, partner, I forgi—" Then, he let out a sigh, and his head flopped back.

Greg watched the light fade from his eyes as the life left his body. He bit back the desire to raise his head and curse. The hot sting of unshed tears clouded his vision.

Damn, he thought. The last thing he did was forgive me.

But, Greg would never forgive himself.

Charles Ray

CHAPTER 3

As they approached the detective division's night duty car, a powder-blue Crown Vic, Greg took the keys from his pocket.

"You wanta drive?" he said. "I'm still not too familiar with the streets here."

He flipped the keys to Meade who smiled as he deftly snagged them from the air.

"No prob, partner. I know every street and back alley in this one-horse shit hole."

Greg had barely buckled in when Meade pushed the gas pedal to the floor, causing the car's enhanced engine to roar. He braced himself with his palms against the padded dash, wary of the radio/computer console mounted just above his left knee in the middle. But, Meade laughed and eased out of their parking slot and drove onto the street behind the police station at a sedate speed.

"You had me worried for a minute there, partner," Greg said. "The way you revved the engine, I thought you were gonna gun it."

"Nah, I just like to hear that throaty sound. I wouldn't drive through the streets like that, though. That kind of driving is for losers."

Greg relaxed in the seat, as best he could when on the way to a crime scene, and, watched the parade of street lights and lit-up store windows go by. As one would expect in a town on the shores of the Chesapeake, many of the stores sold sailing and fishing gear, and most of the restaurants specialized in seafood, with Maryland crab cakes predominant. Despite its population, Darden's urban area was small, and they were soon in the outskirts, where they passed small wood-frame houses, one- and two-story, encircled by a variety of fencing, and many with politically-incorrect black lawn jockeys on their lawns. There were few people of color in most of the towns along the bay, and political correctness consisted of them not using the N-word in Greg's presence. He had little doubt, from the number of signs in support of extreme right-wing political candidates, that that word and other racial epithets were used freely when the conversation group didn't contain people with high melanin content in their skin.

He glanced at Meade out of the corner of his eye. An easy-going type, he seemed okay to Greg, and he didn't detect the undertone of resentment that he sensed from the other detectives, and even some of the uniformed patrol officers, which he could never be sure wasn't based on his being a newcomer who'd taken a job that a local boy should've gotten. The fact that they'd hired Sandra Carter sort of indicated an open-mindedness. Even relegating her mainly to dispatch duties couldn't be faulted on the surface. She was sharp, but not, in Greg's view, physically suited to street duty.

Then, he mentally chided himself. *No sense looking for prejudice. If it's there, it'll rear its ugly head sooner or later, and I'll deal with it then. For now, we have a possible murder case to deal with.* And, he was pretty sure that's what it was. One dead body in a park could be an accidental death, but he was pretty sure that two bodies weren't. He'd have to be sharp. Everyone would be looking at every move he made, every word he uttered.

It wasn't long before they were on the street that led to Raleigh Park, a quiet, wooded park on the lower shelf of a bluff overlooking the bay. The top of the bluff was occupied by the largest building in town, a palatial structure that Meade had pointed out to him during his orientation drive to familiarize himself with Darden, and that Meade identified as Caldecott Manor. When Greg asked for more information, Meade said, "The Caldecott family is beyond rich. They own over half the land in Darden, and over half the mortgages. Well, actually, it's Max Caldecott now. Old man Caldecott died five years ago, leaving Max and his mom. Anyway, they never come out of the castle to mingle with us commoners, and the only people that see them are the few who work for them."

The jumble of trees, dark shapes against the moon-lit sky, came into view, and behind it, like some prehistoric redoubt, Caldecott Manor loomed over everything.

A uniformed officer waited for them at the entrance to the park, and gave Meade directions to the scene, which wasn't hard to find, since the crime scene tech, Hal Goodman, had set up four floodlights to illuminate it. Greg could see Dr. Marcus Stone, one of four doctors in town, who also served as the medical examiner for the police department, squatting in front of a large oak tree. He could just make out four naked legs splayed out in front of Stone.

He and Meade got out of the car and approached the scene, and as the scene in front of Stone became clear, Greg felt his supper threatened to exit via his throat. Beside him, Meade gasped and said, "Holy shit."

The victims were a male and a female who looked to be in their late teens, both nude, with the male on his knees, his butt in the air, bowing with his forehead on the ground between the female's legs, which were splayed out in forming a Y with her body the stem of the letter. Both were completely naked. Looking closer, he could see the ugly gash in the male victim's throat and the stab wound in the center of the female's chest and wondered about the small amount of blood he could see.

Greg took a deep breath and stepped up beside the doctor. Stone looked up at him and smiled grimly.

"What do we have here, doctor?" Greg asked.

"A fucking mess," Stone said. "A total fucking mess. They weren't killed here, as you can probably tell from the amount of blood." He pointed to a clearing in the trees about twenty meters deeper into the park. "Blood over there indicates that was the kill zone, and then the bodies were moved here."

Greg felt a chill in his gut.

"They were staged?"

"Yeah, looks like it."

"What else can you tell me?"

"Not a lot," Stone said. "Time of death, based on lack of rigor, is between 9 and 11 pm, cause of death, Exsanguination . . . that's massive blood loss to the uninitiated, from lacerations with a devilishly sharp instrument. That's all preliminary, though. I won't know for sure until I do an autopsy."

"Any ID on the victims?"

"None. Their clothing and any ID, phones, or anything like that, are gone. I assume the killer took them. It'll take me a while to ID them."

Greg looked down at the bodies. Something about the way they were posed disturbed him. Death was an obscenity, but this was . . . truly bizarre.

"Whoever did this is one sick puppy," he said.

"It gets crazier, detective," Stone said. He knelt and pointed at the female victim's midsection, just before the stab wound in her chest. "See this?"

Greg looked closer. He hadn't noticed at first, taking the markings on the girl's torso as perhaps just scratches, but upon closer inspection, he could see that letters had been carved into her flesh, probably with the same weapon that had been used to stab her. After a few seconds the scratched letters became clear, and he felt like someone had kicked him in the stomach.

In precise block letters, someone had carved,

It is good for a man not to touch a woman

"What the fuck! Was this done post- or peri-mortem, doc?"

"Looks to be post-mortem. And, from the neatness and alignment of the letters, the killer took his bloody time doing it."

Greg shook his head. He looked at his partner "We are dealin' with one sick motherfucker here, partner. As of this moment, all time off's canceled. We're not resting until this sick fuck's in a cell or in the morgue."

Meade, with a serious expression on his face for once, nodded. "You got that right. Let's find this dickhead."

Charles Ray

CHAPTER 4

Greg and Meade had the uniforms do a wide sweep of the area around where the bodies were found, but, other than the blood-soaked area where Dr. Stone figured the two were killed, nothing was found. There were no residences or business nearby, and they saw no signs of anyone else having in or near the park, so he had a single patrol car cruise the area just in case, but otherwise felt that a canvas of the area looking for witnesses was a waste of time.

Once Stone cleared the bodies to be moved and the morgue wagon had carted them off, the two detectives went back to the station, where they found David Hoag, Darden's chief of police, wearing a rumpled Baltimore Ravens sweat shirt and faded jeans, perched on the corner of Greg's desk. His chin was covered with morning stubble and he had dark circles under his sad brown eyes.

Hoag glanced at his watch as they approached.

"How bad is it?" he asked.

Greg had found Hoag's habit of launching right into business, and sometimes starting a conversation in the middle rather than some logical beginning, both refreshing and unsettling. It was refreshing in that he didn't feel the need to beat around the bush with the man, but unsettling, because it was often difficult to figure out exactly what he was getting at until you'd talked for a while.

This time, though, he knew exactly what Hoag wanted to know.

"Pretty bad, chief," he said. "Two vics, male and female, late teens, early twenties. Male had his throat cut, female stabbed in the chest, and the bodies were moved from the kill site and staged. Female had a message carved into her stomach, 'The Bad Also Die Young.' No witnesses, and no apparent trace evidence at the scene."

Hoag's face paled. "Shit. Any ID on the victims?"

"Doc Stone said he'd get us something by mid-morning." Greg looked at his watch. It was now 4:30 am. *Where the hell did the night go? Seems like just an hour or so ago I was pissed at my partner for being late, and now our official shift's almost over.* You want Meade and me to wait for that to come in?"

Hoag rubbed at the stubble on his chin, making a rasping sound. He shook his head.

"Nah, when your shift's over at 6:30, go home and get some sleep. The two of you are off night shift duty for the time being. I want you to focus on solving this case."

"Okay, chief." Greg turned to Meade. "I guess the first thing we need to do is set up a chart of some kind to keep track of the case."

Meade smiled. "You mean like they do on TV?"

"Yeah, just like on TV. Sometimes, Hollywood gets it right, and it just happens to be a good way to sort things out."

Meade had a look on his face like a puppy watching its owner head for the leash on the hook by the door. The only thing missing, Greg thought, was a lolling tongue hanging out of his mouth.

"Wow," Meade said. "I never worked a murder case before. I figure you must've done a few when you were on the force in DC, right?"

"More than I care to remember," Greg said.

A throat-clearing sound pulled their attention back to Hoag, who was still perched on the corner of Greg's desk.

"Anything else, chief?" Greg hoped the answer would be, 'no, keep up the good work,' but he wouldn't be so lucky.

"I know I don't need to tell you how important it is that you get this case wrapped up quickly," Hoag said.

"We'll do our best, chief."

"You've got to do more than your best, Greg. Besides the fishing industry, the only thing this damn town has got going is tourism, and murder, especially an unsolved murder, is bad for tourism. You get my drift?"

He got the message all right, and he understood why the police chief was in the building at 4:00 in the morning dressed like he'd just come from a frat party.

"The mayor's on your back, right?"

Carlton Pruitt, the six-term mayor of Darden, whose father had been mayor before him, was a consummate politician. Good for kissing babies, doing favors, and little else. He also owned two of the six charter fishing boat companies in town. So, Greg surmised, it was a good bet he'd heard about the bodies and had called the police chief with instructions to make sure they didn't interfere with his business.

Hoag winced at Greg's remark.

"Oh, Mayor Pruitt's okay . . . for a politician," he said. "And, he only has the town's best interests at heart."

Right. And, pigs fly. "Don't worry, chief," Greg said. "We're all over this case like flies on shit, and we'll nail this perp as quickly as we can."

"Good man. I knew I made the right choice hiring you."

Leaving that remark hanging in the air like a fart in a closed room, Hoag hoisted himself off the desk and walked out.

Greg shook himself and turned to Meade again.

"We got a white board around here somewhere?"

"Yeah. There's one in the supply room they use for training. Want me to get it?"

No, I want you to toss it off the roof. Of course, I want you to get it, dumb ass, is what Greg thought and wanted to say, but instead, he said, "Yeah, if you would. And, set it up between our desks. I'll start pulling together the information we have.

As Meade went off toward the supply room in the rear of the building, Greg sat down and pulled out his notebook. He looked at his crabby writing and realized that he really had nothing but two bodies and a whole lot of speculation. As he looked at the bottom of the last page where he'd written the note carved on the woman's belly and got a creepy sensation at the base of his skull. *Don't jump to conclusions. Follow the evidence.*

Meade came back with a large white board on a green metal easel, which he set up in the passageway beside their desks. He'd also found a box containing dry markers and one with the little yellow sticky notes. He took out a black marker and wrote **DEATHS IN RALEIGH PARK** at the top center of the board. He had written **VIC** at the top left corner when a uniformed patrolman came into the bullpen leading an elderly man wearing an overcoat despite the warm weather and leading a Scottish Terrier on a frayed leather leash.

"Hey, Ronnie," Meade said. "Whatcha got there?"

"'S'up, Larry, Detective Kildare," the cop said. "I was making a last sweep around the park when I ran into Mr. Jarvis here. He was out walkin' his dog around the time of the murders, 'n he said he might've got a look at our perp."

Greg's pulse rate picked up. He couldn't believe their luck. A witness could make the difference in this case being closed or cold. He stood and motioned at the empty chair beside his desk.

"That's great," he said. "Why don't you have a seat Mr. Jarvis. Would you like a cup of coffee?"

The old man squinted at Greg. "Sure, I could use a cup." He eased himself into the chair and patted his left knee. The terrier moved until its body was against the man's leg and then sat, eying Greg with its tongue lolling out of the side of its mouth.

"Just sit tight, sir," Greg said. "I'll be right back."

He went to the cubby at the rear of the bullpen and filled a white mug with the tarry-looking coffee that had been sitting since his night shift began. He grabbed two packets of sugar and one of cream powder and returned to his desk, where he put the coffee and the three packets on the desk near the old man.

Slowly and deliberately, the old man picked up the packets and tore them open. He then dumped the contents into the coffee. The cream floated on top of the dark brown liquid for a few seconds, slowly dissolving. After it was just a beige spot on the surface of the coffee, the old man picked the cup up, blew on it, and then took a sip. He grimaced, and then took a bigger swallow.

"Thank you, young fella," he said.

"Sorry about the coffee," Greg said. "But, it's all we have at the moment."

"It's not too bad." As if to validate his statement, he took another sip.

"It's hot, and nice and strong, just the way I like it."

Greg took out his notebook and pen and opened the notebook on the desk. "Now, sir, if you'd give me your full name and address."

"Name's Bradley Jarvis," the man said. "I live at 5541 Maple Lane, about a mile from Raleigh Park."

"And, you were in the park last night around nine or ten?"

"Yeah, I was. Lobo here had to do his business, and he needed some exercise." He patted the dog's head.

"Isn't that a bit late to walk so far to take your dog out?"

"Son, when you get to be my age, you don't sleep all that much. Ain't got all that much time left, and I get bored living all alone, so I walk a lot late at night."

The old man was smiling as he talked, so Greg returned the smile.

"Yeah, I can understand that," he said. "I live alone myself, and sometimes I like to walk late at night to clear my head. So, tell me what you saw or heard last night."

"I have to tell you up front, young fella, my eyesight's not so good, so I can't be absolutely sure about what I saw."

"I understand. Just take your time and tell me the best you can."

"Okay. I can do that." Jarvis patted his dog's head again. "Like I said, Lobo and me were taking our nightly constitutional, and something spooked him. Sometimes squirrels or groundhogs get his attention, but he just chases 'em. But, this time, he looked really spooked. Just stopped on the trail with his tail straight out and the hairs on his neck standing on end."

"Something he heard scared him?"

"Maybe, or something he smelled. When that there young cop told me what'd happened in the park, I figured it was probably the blood he smelled. Dogs got sharp noses, you know. Anyway, he's standing there quivering and looking into the woods. Kinda started gettin' to me, too, you know. I figured maybe we ought to turn around and go home, 'n I was just about to do that when I saw this figure come out of the trees down the path from where I was standing. I knelt down and petted Lobo to keep 'im from barking. He's well trained. Stayed quiet as you please, just standing there all stiff legged."

"What time did you see this figure?"

"Not sure, but it musta been close on to 10:30, maybe even 11:00, 'cause I left home at a quarter to nine, and it takes me an hour or so to get to the park."

Greg made a note on his pad.

"Can you describe the figure you saw?"

"Now, I told you, my eyesight ain't so good. All I could tell is that it looked like a man, all dressed in black. He was about your size, and he was carrying something folded under his arms. Never got a look at his face, 'cause he tried to stay in the shadows."

"Which way did he go?"

"He was headin' toward the entrance to the park. Let me tell you, it was kinda spooky. I just stood there for about twenty minutes, until I was sure he wasn't coming back, then I headed out of the park myself."

"How did the police officer find you?"

"Well, I was headin' home, but Lobo hadn't finished his business, so I got off the street and went in the woods a little ways and let him do his thing. He likes to play around a little after, so I reckon we musta been in them woods for near on to an hour. I was comin' out and headin' home when the police car stopped next to me, and that young fellow asked me if I'd been anywhere near the park between nine and eleven. When I said I did, and asked why, he told me they'd found somebody killed there, and he wanted to know if I'd seen or heard anything. Well, I told him what I just told you, 'n he asked me to get in the car and come in and make a statement to the detective in charge, so here I am. Was what I give you helpful?"

Other than sort of confirming that the perp was likely a man, and that, as Greg had suspected, he'd taken the victims' possessions with him, it wasn't really much help. But, Greg said, "You have been very helpful, Mr. Jarvis. If there were more citizens like you, we'd solve more crimes a lot quicker."

"Glad to be of help. That young cop said the ones killed was kids, is that true?"

"I can't go into details regarding an ongoing investigation, sir, but I will say that they did appear to be quite young."

"Aw, that's terrible. There's just so much violence these days involving young folks. I wonder sometimes what the world's comin' to."

"True. Well, thank you for your assistance. I'll have the patrol officer take you and Lobo home."

After Jarvis and his dog were gone, Greg went to the white board and wrote,

SUSPECT??
Male, 6 ft, 190 lb., dark clothing

He then finished Meade's entry,

VICTIMS

1. Male –
2. Female -

"Not a lot to go on," Meade said.

"True that." Greg nodded. "But, it's a start."

CHAPTER 5

They sat and stared at the whiteboard for several minutes, each lost in his own thoughts.

Finally, Greg sat forward. "You know, Larry, I'm getting a bad feeling about this case."

"Yeah, me too. Bad enough it's my first murder case, but the way they were killed is . . . icky."

Despite himself, Greg laughed. Meade was the only adult he knew who would use the word 'icky.'

"There's that, but it's the staging of the bodies, the removal of all their possessions, and the apparent lack of forensic evidence that bothers me."

"That *will* make it a bitch to catch this guy; and having the chief and the mayor breathin' down our backs ain't gonna help either."

Greg nodded. "And, what's worse is, I think this guy's gonna kill again."

Meade's eyes widened and his mouth flopped open.

"Wha-! What the hell makes you say that? You psychic or something?"

"No, I'm not psychic. But, I have had training in investigating unusual homicides. I'll tell you what I think about this perp. He's organized, and he's focused. Did you notice; other than the slashed throat and the stab wound in the chest, there didn't appear to be any other damage. This is a guy who knows how to kill. He probably stalked them before attacking, and he's good; he got them both without any apparent signs of a struggle or effort to defend themselves. And, that staging of the bodies and the message carved in that girl's stomach. I tell you, Larry, we got ourselves a psycho here, and he *will* kill again if we don't stop him."

Meade looked at him, his expression hard to read. Then, he shook his head.

"Partner, if I'm hearing you right, you just described a psychopathic serial or spree killer."

Greg nodded. "It has the signs of one."

"Well, Greg, I know you're the boss 'n all, but lemme clue you in on something you need to know if you're gonna be a cop in this town. You never, and I mean never, use the term serial killer around Chief Hoag."

"Why the hell not?"

"Because, if we have a serial killer, he'll feel obligated to tell Anne Arundel County, and they'll probably call in the state cops for help, and when that happens the feebs won't be far behind. And, if there's one thing Hoag hates more than workin' with state cops, it's workin' with the FBI."

"But, dammit, if we do have a serial killer, and I think we do, we need all the help we can get."

"I'm just sayin', partner. But, if we involve the FBI, the mayor's gonna have puppies. You know how the feds are. They like holdin' press conferences and crowin' about how good they are. That would put the tourist trade in town in the toilet, and the mayor won't like that at all. Now, I ain't supposed to be tellin' you this, but you gotta know. Hoag went out on a limb hirin' you. The mayor was against it. Dave Pruitt's his cousin on his father's side, and he's got the most seniority of us detectives. The mayor wanted him to have the job."

"Shit," Greg said. "So, in order to keep my job, I have to do it in a half-assed way."

Meade chuckled. "Half-assed is better than no ass, and if you cause the feds to come in, the mayor will insist that Hoag rip your ass off."

Greg blew air through his nose.

"This won't be easy."

"Never thought it would," Meade said. "But, I got your back."

"Why would you put yourself out for an outsider? After all, weren't you also under consideration for this job?"

"Yeah, as was every detective here. But, the difference is, I got no high-powered relatives pushing my case, and knew goin' in I didn't have a snowball's chance in hell of bein' selected. Besides, as partners go, you're not too shabby, and partners look out for each other, right?"

Greg felt a twinge of guilt as Meade's words brought Tony Nunez to mind. He shook it off.

"Shit, I guess that's part of bein' on a small-town police force. I never had to play politics in DC, because I was too low in the food chain."

"Well, you've come up in the world, partner," Meade said. "But, don't forget that there are a couple of predators higher in the chain than you."

Greg shook his head. "If this wasn't such a beautiful little town, I'd say the hell with it. But, I kinda like it here, so I reckon I'll have to play the game." He slapped his hand on his desk, rattling the cup of pens and pencils he kept near the phone. "Okay, let's see if we can nail this son of a bitch before he kills again."

Charles Ray

CHAPTER 6

While Meade's information was news to Greg, he wasn't particularly surprised. Hoag was always hinting that hiring him had been a risk, and the one time he'd met Mayor Pruitt, he'd sensed that the man didn't like him very much. Now, he knew why.

That was all a distraction, though. He was sure in his mind that a serial killer was on the prowl in Arden and was determined to catch him. He didn't want a repeat of the subway killer.

- - -

He'd only had his detective shield for a month when the first body was found. One of the homeless men who panhandled near the Dupont Circle Metro Station had been found in an alley off Church Street, two blocks from the station at the start of the morning rush hour. Because it was winter, it was first thought that the old man, a drug addict and wino, had frozen to death, but when the M.E. examined the corpse, he discovered that the man had been strangled with what looked like an extension cord. The death of a homeless person wasn't a high priority for the department, so the case was assigned to him, the rookie and newest addition to the homicide division.

After leaving the chief's office, he immediately sought out the detective who was supposed to be mentoring him, Detective Sergeant John Carson. A 25-year veteran of the DC police, and nearing retirement, Carson had at one time been a rising star. But, too many mutilated corpses in alleys, followed by trips down the neck of a bottle of cheap whiskey, had sidelined him. Sergeant was as high as he would go. Greg didn't think there was much he could learn from the man, but this was his first case, and he wanted to do well. He figured that Carson would at least be able to provide him with a few tips on the best way to conduct it.

He was surprised, therefore, when, after explaining the case, Carson cocked his head to one side and rubbed the stubble on his jaw. "You wanta know what I'd do, kid?"

"I sure do, detective," Greg said. "This is my first case, and I want to get it right, you know."

"Well, for starters, kid, stop callin' me detective. You're my partner for a while, so you might as well call me John or Johnny. Don't make no never mind to me which. Then, here's how you handle this case. You go to the scene and take lots of notes. Then you look around and see if there might be a witness or two. These bums are loners, but there's usually three or four of them around any area. You ask them if they saw anything, they say they didn't see nothing, you write that down, then you come back and put your notes in the file. After a while, unless whoever did it comes in and confesses, it goes to the cold case files."

"Surely there's more to it than that?"

"Naw, kid. DC's got a high murder rate, and we just don't have the resources to go balls to the wall on every one of 'em. A homeless drunk ain't gonna rank high on anybody's priority list. That's just the way it is."

Greg felt deflated. What Carson said made sense, but it was the wrong kind of sense. It put a value on human life, with some in the high brackets, some in the low. What he was hearing was that the homeless were in the 'no-value' bracket. Well, he wouldn't just brush it aside. He would give it his best shot. One way or another, he would make an impact on the entrenched bureaucrats in the department, starting with his erstwhile mentor.

"Tell you what . . . John; I won't call you detective if you'll stop callin' me kid. My name, in case you forgot, is Greg."

Carson laughed. "Okay, Greg. Good to see you're capable of barking back. Good luck with the case. I'd go out with you, but all that dust in alleys aggravates my asthma. But, then, you were tops in your academy class, and have a pretty good record from your time in uniform, so you really shouldn't need me."

Greg was just happy not to have him along. He didn't need his cynical attitude.

He checked a car out of the department motor pool and drove to the scene on Church Street. The crime scene tape, except for a few torn fragments, had been removed shortly after the body was taken away. The alley looked like all the other alleys he'd seen during his time on the force; dumpsters overflowing with the detritus of the offices, apartments and townhouses in the area, treasure troves for the legions of homeless men and women who roamed the streets day and night, surviving on handouts, what they could find dumpster diving, and a lot of luck. The surface was unpaved, covered with a layer of fine gravel that crunched under his shoes as he made his way to the grease-covered dumpster against the responding officer's report said he'd been left sitting.

Standing in front of the trash receptacle, he did a slow 360, taking in the atmosphere of the place. But, nothing spoke to him. He was wondering if the homeless man's killer had lain in wait for him behind the dumpster, and if the victim had been alone in this dreary place except for his killer. Then, he saw movement out of the corner of his left eye, near the farthest dumpster from the street.

A large cardboard panel moved, first up, and then to the side, and a grimy hand emerged from beneath it. The hand was followed by an arm clad in a frayed brown jacket, and then a shoulder, and finally a head and an upper body. The man's face was so grimy and dirty, if not for his flyaway hair which was the color of hay that has lain on a stable floor and been coated with manure, he wouldn't have even been able to tell his race. The homeless society, in a city that was eighty percent black but still highly segregated in its housing, was the only truly integrated element of the national capital. Most of the homeless, many of them drug addicts or alcoholics, and most with severe mental conditions, had begun appearing in great numbers all over the city shortly after Ronald Reagan became president and axed the federal mental health funding to local mental institutions that had been championed by Jimmy Carter. Without funding, many patients were sent to locally-funded halfway houses, but most ended up on the streets. Because of the year-round warm weather, West Coast cities like Los Angeles saw a boom in homeless on their streets, but despite sweltering summers and arctic winters caused by the excessive humidity in the city, Washington, DC also saw a large increase in homeless men and women sitting on street corners, sleeping on park benches or over steam grates, throughout the city, but with a preference for those areas where government workers, politicians and lobbyists worked, because it they got larger handouts. In the late 1990s and early 2000s, homeless grifters started accosting passengers on the Metro, the area's subway line, hanging around at station entrances, and even bumming enough change to buy a ticket and working the station platforms or the train cars.

As the man slowly crawled from beneath the cardboard he stretched and yawned, showing a mouth only half full of crooked, tobacco-stained teeth. Greg's hand went to the butt of his service weapon in a reflex action, even though he knew it was unlikely the man would do anything more than try and bum a few bucks off him. His face felt hot as he shook his hand and pulled it away from his Glock.

Sure enough, when the man's eyes focused, and he saw Greg standing there in his clean blue suit and shiny black shoes, he smiled and stood. Greg forced himself not to back away as the man approached, and as he got closer and the reek of a body that hadn't been washed in a long time caused his eyes to sting, he reconsidered backing away very seriously before reminding himself that he was here to investigate a murder and this might be a witness.

"Hey, brother man, ya got any spare change?" the man asked, holding out a grimy hand.

Greg reached inside his jacket. But, instead of change, he pulled out his badge and held it up so the man could see.

"I might have a dollar or two," he said. "But, first, I'd like to ask you a few questions."

"Damn. So, I gots to sing for my supper. Okay, whatcha wanna know?"

"There was a man found dead here, he was killed last night or early this morning. I-"

"You mean old sneaky Pete," the man said, cutting Greg off. Yeah, I know he got himself offed."

"Sneaky Pete? That's his name? You knew him?"

"Hell, man, everybody on the street knew sneaky Pete."

"You know his last name?"

"Naw. We don't use last names down here on the street. Ain't got no need for 'em, you know."

"Why was he called sneaky Pete?" Greg was thinking maybe the victim was a thief and had probably crossed someone.

"We call him that 'cause he was in the war, the Vietnam War. He was one of them commandos or something, you know. Got a bad case of that post-something-stress—"

"Post-traumatic Stress Disorder," Greg said. "PTSD."

"Yeah, that. He had it bad. Couldn't hold a job, 'n sometimes he'd get so down, he'd just crawl in a bottle of hooch and not come out for days. He was in a special hospital until the government cut the money, 'n they kicked him out."

Shit, Greg thought, *the victim was a veteran. We can send people all over the fucking planet to wage wars but can't do shit for 'em when they come back home with their minds and bodies broken.* "You know anyone who'd want to do him harm?"

"Sneaky Pete? Naw, man. The dude was as gentle as a lamb, 'n he'd give you the shirt off his back. Ain't nobody down here'd hurt Pete."

"Did you happen to be in the alley last night or this morning?"

"Naw, I come in after the cops left. I spent last night over to Foggy Bottom."

So much for the thief pissing someone off theory. Now Greg was left with a dilemma. If it wasn't someone with a grudge, why would anyone kill a homeless drunk, and by strangulation, no less. It made no sense—unless—he remembered a class at the academy when an agent from the FBI had come in and lectured them on psychopaths, in particular, serial killers; some people who killed because voices in their head ordered them to, and others who did for the sheer joy of killing. The problem was that the agent had told them that it's not officially a serial killer case until there are three bodies. His description of how they worked, though, triggered thoughts in Greg's mind. And, this case fit some of them. A killing that on the surface seemed senseless, no apparent motive, and no forensic evidence left on the victim or at the scene. Whoever did it had been meticulous—the hallmark of a serial killer.

As much as he disliked talking to Carson, he couldn't wait to get back to the station to talk to him.

He should have, he decided later, have saved himself the trouble. Carson listened to his theory, and after he'd finished, laughed for a full two minutes until he had tears in his eyes and was holding his side. He then spent another ten minutes debunking Greg's theory and urging him to file his report and move on.

He filed his report, but couldn't get the case out of his mind, and then, six days later, another body was found near a Metro station, this time Congress Heights in Anacostia, and it wasn't a homeless person, but a middle-aged woman who worked as a janitor at the Kennedy Center, heading home after work on the last train of the evening. Her body was found by the station crew when they came to work the following day to open the station. She'd been strangled and stuffed behind a bank of newspaper dispensers near the station entrance.

When Greg heard about the case, he went to see the M.E., and was told that the ligature marks on the woman's neck were similar to those on the homeless man, but because the incidents were so far apart, it was likely a coincidence.

No one wanted to accept that a psycho was on the loose, and no one would listen to Greg's theories. Until, the third body was found, again a homeless man, behind the strip mall adjacent to the Cleveland Park Metro Station. When the marks on the man's neck matched the first two victims, people started listening, even Carson. More detectives were thrown at the case, working around the clock, but there were still six more victims, nine in all, before they identified and arrested the killer, a former attendant at a mental institution who'd been fired for having inappropriate contact with a female patient. When he was interrogated, he confessed that he'd always had the urge to kill, but until he was canned, he'd restricted it to stray animals. But, after he was let go from the only job he'd ever had in his life, he just snapped, and upped his game to people. He said, it made him feel important, and helped him get through the day.

The man, a thin, narrow-faced individual you could pass on the street a thousand times and never notice, showed absolutely no remorse, and described his killings as dispassionately as if he'd been talking about clipping hedges.

Greg had trouble sleeping for weeks afterward. The only plus side to the whole thing was that his stock went up dramatically in the department. Being the lone wolf to recognize what everyone else missed, or ignored, set him apart from his colleagues, and from that moment on, until the day Nunez was killed, he was given the really hard cases, and his closure rate was as close to a hundred percent as you can get. He'd failed to solve one case because the suspect he was pursuing committed suicide, leaving a note to Greg, saying that he did it because he wanted to see him fail for once. Even though Greg had the man in his sights for a week before he killed himself, he refused to accept credit for closing the case.

– ▪ ▪ ▪

And, here he was again, knowing what he had but unable to convince anyone else.

So, he would play their game—up to a point. At the end of the day, though, as much as he liked living in Darden, he would do what was right.

CHAPTER 7

The sound of fingers snapping caused him to jerk forward in his chair.

"Hey, Earth to Greg," Meade said. "You were off somewhere in la-la land, partner. You okay?"

Greg blinked and shook himself. "Yeah, I'm fine," he said. "I was just thinking about this case."

Meade looked at the whiteboard and the paucity of evidence on it. "How do you want to do it?" he asked.

"Well, first we need to ID the victims. Then we do a deep dive into their backgrounds to see if that gives us a clue as to who might want to kill them."

Meade nodded.

"That's as good a place as any to start," he said. "Doc Stone probably won't have anything until this afternoon, though."

Greg yawned. He suddenly realized that he was on the verge of falling asleep at his desk. He glanced at his watch. Ten minutes until end of shift. The time, which for a while had seemed to be moving at the pace of a glacier, had, without warning, picked up the pace and somehow zipped by without him noticing.

"First thing we do is go home and get some shut-eye. Then, we come back this afternoon and hit it fresh. In addition to whatever we can get from the doc,

47

we need to go back and take another look at the crime scene, both the kill site and the place where the bodies were placed."

"You really think that'll do any good?"

"Yeah, I do. I don't know how to explain it, Larry, but sometimes crime scenes talk to me." At his partner's wide-eyed look, he held his hands up in a gesture of surrender. "Hey, I don't mean literally talk, like hearing voices, but when I walk some crime scenes, I get impressions of what happened. I guess you could say I pick up the residual negative energy of the place."

Meade cocked his head to the side and stared at him through narrow slits. "O-o-okay, whatever floats your boat. I guess big-city policing is different from the way we do it out here in the sticks."

"Okay, I know it sounds crazy," Greg said. "But, come along with me and I'll show you how I do it. The other thing we need to do is follow up with the patrols to see if they found any other witnesses."

"Yeah, somebody better than old man Jarvis. You know he's legally blind, right? Can't see more'n twenty feet in front, and that's probably fuzzy."

Greg nodded.

"He did say up front that his eyesight wasn't so good, but, yeah, I noticed he seemed to be sort of unfocused, a sign of someone who can't see, and he kept petting his dog's head without looking at it. Oh, and that dog sat there and never made a sound or reacted in any way to people coming and going. A sure sign of a service animal."

Looking impressed, Meade said, "Pretty good. I didn't think you were paying attention."

"Hey, that's what we detectives do; we detect."

Okay, hotshot, if you're such a good detective, tell me what I'm thinking right now."

Greg looked at his watch again. "You're thinking it's a minute past end of shift, and we're sitting here jerking off instead of heading home to get some sleep."

"Well, I'll be stripped and dipped in a crab pot," Meade said. "You *do* read minds."

Charles Ray

CHAPTER 8

Greg went home to the little New England cottage he was renting, surrounded by a white picket fence, on Wisteria Street, a cul-de-sac in a little bedroom community on the south side of Darden, not far from Raleigh Park, and, after a desultory shower to wash the grime of the night shift from his eyes, fell into bed.

He woke up after six hours, opened one eye, and noted that the clock on his bedside table read 1:15. He rolled off the bed, padded to the bathroom, and went through the motions like an automaton until the sting of icy water from the shower hit his face, waking him the rest of the way.

After getting dressed, he made a peanut butter and fried spam on toasted whole wheat bread sandwich, wrapped it in wax paper and with a can of orange soda clutched in his left hand, left his house for the short drive to police headquarters. He put the soda in the cup holder and the unwrapped sandwich on the passenger seat of his 2013 Toyota 4-Runner and alternated between sandwich and drink as he drove one-handed along Darden's uncrowded streets. He smiled at the thought of doing something like that in DC's traffic at almost any time of the day. It would be suicide at worst or lead to a fender bender at best.

By the time he pulled his 4-Runner into the parking spot behind headquarters reserved for him as chief of detectives, he'd finished his meal. He wrapped the wax paper around the soda can and dropped them into the recycle bin just inside the door to the building.

For once, Meade had beaten him to work. When he entered the bullpen, he found his partner sitting at his desk staring at the whiteboard.

"Any ideas coming at you from staring at that nearly empty board?" he asked.

Meade gave him a sour look.

"Hell, no. I thought I'd try and see if I could get what little evidence we got to talk to me, but all I get is silence."

Greg laughed. "Maybe you're trying too hard. It's like meditating. People who strain to clear their thoughts end up thinking harder. You have to relax and let your *chi* flow."

"Let my *what* flow?"

"Your *chi*. That's the fundamental life force or energy. It flows through everything. When you release your *chi* to float freely, it can integrate with the *chi* of your surroundings. That's how you get a crime scene to talk to you—at least, it's how I do it."

"Damn, man, you're a bundle of surprises. A mind reader *and* an Indian Yogi. What other secrets are you hiding from me, partner?"

Greg couldn't tell if his partner was kidding or serious, but he was saved from having to respond to him by the shrill buzz of his phone.

"Detective Kildare," he said into the mouthpiece. "How may I help you?"

"This is Marcus Stone. I figured you guys would want some results as soon as possible, so I fast-tracked the autopsies of our two victims."

"Great, doc. Whatcha got?"

"I'd rather give it to you face-to-face," Stone said. "I don't like discussing cases over the phone. When can you come to my office?"

"Be there in fifteen minutes," he said, and hung up the phone. He smiled at Meade. "That was Doc Stone. He has the autopsy results on our vics."

Meade stood. "Good, maybe he found something that'll help us figure out who this bastard is. Let's go see what the sawbones can tell us."

He moved toward the door. Still smiling, Greg followed.

Bayshore Hospital, where Stone was the chief surgeon and majority owner, was located on State Route 261, a five-minute drive south of town. Greg, though, had a thing about being on time or early, so he routinely added five to ten minutes to his estimated travel time, a habit which amused his new partner to no end. Meade was even more tickled when Greg insisted on driving, saying that it was about time he started learning his way around.

Not that he could've missed the hospital. Despite not being much bigger than some of the emergency care clinics in the DC area, it was the most prominent building in the area it occupied, its neighbors being a crab restaurant across the road and a junkyard a few hundred meters further south on the same side. It was where the town's four doctors did their work. Stone had converted part of the hospital's morgue into a medical examiner's office, with a viewing room, a file room for police-related cases, and a small office where he conducted any police business.

Greg and Meade found him seated behind a battered old gray steel desk that looked like it had been picked up at a defense surplus auction. He had two manila folders on the desk.

"Come in, gentlemen," he said. "Pull up chairs." He waved at two folding metal chairs, one to either side of the desk.

"Whatcha got, doc?" Meade said. "And, please, give it to us in English, not that gobbledygook you doctors like to use."

Stone frowned, but there was a look of merriment in his eyes. "You guys take all the fun out of this. I should've insisted you come and view the procedure. That's the last time I play nice with you."

"I wouldn't have minded, doc," Greg said. "When I worked in DC, I routinely observed autopsies."

"Don't pay my partner any attention," Meade said. "I think he's a bit . . . you know." He made circular motions at his temple with his forefinger. "You know he reads minds?"

"Is that so?" Meade looked at him with half-closed eyes. "Can you tell me what I'm thinking?"

"Hey, doc, he's just pulling your leg. I can't read minds."

"Darn. I could've used the entertainment. Well, I suppose you want to know what I found, right?"

Greg bit back a biting remark. He was never quite sure how much of the banter he witnessed, especially from and between Stone and Meade, was just that, banter, and how much of it was a passive aggressive way of expressing their feelings about him, an outsider, invading their little community.

"Yeah, if you don't mind," he said, figuring that was a nice neutral response.

"Okay," Stone said, opening the two folders. "Both victims died of exsanguination. The male from a slashing left to right of the throat that severed both carotid arteries. Death was pretty much immediate from the blood loss. The female died from a single stab wound to the upper chest that nicked her aorta. She probably took nearly a minute to die."

"Shit," Meade said. "That's pretty gruesome. The perp must've been drenched with their blood."

"Maybe, maybe not. The male's wounds look to have been made from behind by a right-handed killer.

The blood would've spurted forward, so except for his hand and arms, he might not've got much on him. There were traces of his blood on the female, so he was facing her when he was cut. And, from where the blood was found, I'd say she was in a . . . state of undress at the time."

"You mean, they were getting it on," Meade said.

Stone frowned at him again. "You, young man, have a dirty mind." He turned back to Greg. "Now, neither victim had any defensive wounds, which tells me our killer struck quickly and decisively, killing the male, whose name, by the way, is Tommy Wakefield, first, and then the female, Belinda Cavanaugh."

Greg pulled out his notebook and wrote down the names. "How were you able to identify them so quickly?" he asked.

"This is a small town, Detective Kildare. I'd fingerprinted them and called for one of the orderlies to take them over to your headquarters. He recognized them. Apparently, they were freshmen the year he graduated from the local high school. They are, were, something of an item. Tommy was the quarterback on the football team, and Belinda was the head cheerleader."

Greg, surprised at first, quickly realized that this wasn't DC, where people often didn't even know the names of their long-time next-door neighbors. That the doctor would not only have learned the victims' names, but knew personal details about them, was part of small-town life that both aided and frustrated police work.

"Okay," he said. "So, you say the killer's right-handed. I assume that's because of the directionality of the throat wound?"

Stone nodded. "And, if I had to guess, I'd say he's either a hunter, a butcher, or a doctor . . . although, I know all the doctors in town, and none of them would do a thing like this. As for hunters, hell, just about every man in town, and a large number of the women hunt, especially in duck season, so good luck with winnowing *that* suspect list down. As for butchers, I know four or five, but most of them are old and fat. This killer is fit and strong, and he's accomplished at his craft."

"What makes you say that?"

"There's no sign of hesitation on the throat wound. I mean, slashing a person's throat is not as easy as they make it look on TV, and most people hesitate when they make the initial cut. In this one, there's not the slightest sign of hesitation. He's done this before, if not on a person, on an animal, like a deer or other small game. Furthermore, Belinda Cavanaugh's wound was a single thrust to the chest that pierced the aorta. That just had to be someone who is familiar with the human body, and again, there was no hesitation."

"Could it be someone just passing through?" Greg didn't believe that, but felt he had to ask.

"Why?" Stone asked. "What stranger would come to a small town like Darden and kill a couple in the park? I mean, it's July, so we have a lot of tourists in town, but most of them are families or couples, here for the charter fishing or touring the docks to watch the watermen at work. Raleigh Park isn't exactly a tourist attraction. I don't think it's even marked on the tourist maps, and I've never seen a tourist there."

Greg was grateful for that, and felt guilty at the emotion, but, trying to find a killer in the transient tourist population would be impossible. In addition, he'd been thinking from his first look at the crime scene that it was someone local who knew the ground. Of course, eliminating the extremely old and very young, that still left somewhere in the neighborhood of three to four thousand potential suspects.

From the sour look on Meade's face, he knew that his partner was probably thinking the same thing.

"Shit," Meade said. "So, what does that leave us to investigate, every physically fit man in town?"

Stone chuckled. "Don't forget the people who live out in the countryside, outside the city limits."

Meade grimaced at the doctor. "Thanks, doc," he said. "You're just a fount of good news today."

Charles Ray

CHAPTER 9

Hal Burns and Janet Croft sat in the front seat of his silver Mercedes 500S sedan, awkwardly groping at each other's clothing, hampered by the console between the seats.

"We could get in the back seat," he said. "There's no console there."

"I'm not climbing over the back of the seat," she said.

"You don't have to climb over. We can get out and get back in."

She looked over her shoulder through the side window, open about eight inches, and all she could see was dark sky with darker trees silhouetted against it.

"No way am I getting out this car out here," she said. "Who knows what kind of animal's out there in the dark?"

He puffed his cheeks out in frustration. Hell, he thought, if I wanted to go through this shit, I'd go home to my wife. Of course, he would never say that aloud. Janet Croft was the best piece of ass in Darden, and no way was he going to queer his first time with her. Man, if only that lump of a husband of hers knew what he was missing, working late every night at his hardware store.

"I have an idea," he said. "There's a way we can do this, and you can stay on your side of the seat, and me on mine."

When she looked confused, he pointed at his crotch and then at her mouth. She frowned.

"Yeah, that's just great for you," she said. "But, what about me?"

He hadn't thought about that. Oh, what the hell, he thought. Might as well.

"Okay," I'll do you first, then you do me."

"Now, I can get down on that," she said, then, realizing what she'd just said, she laughed.

Now, it was his turn to look confused. "What's so funny?"

"I just said I can get down on that. Don't you get it?"

He'd been so obsessed with getting into her pants, his big head had gone to sleep to let his little head have a greater blood supply, but, when prompted, he got it. "Oh, yeah, get down on it. I get it. I can get down on it, too."

He laughed, which made her laugh again, which complicated her efforts to remove her underwear. He helped, which got them all tangled up again, which caused her to start laughing again. Her laughter stopped suddenly when he slipped her panties over her ankles and lowered his head into her lap.

"O-o-o-Oh, yes," she said. "Now, *that* is getting down on it."

They were both so involved in what they were doing, or more accurately, what he was doing to her, they didn't see or hear the black-clad figure approach to within six feet of the car. They were oblivious to him raising the Winchester .30-06 to his shoulder and aiming it at them. They didn't hear his sharp intake of breath as he sucked in lungsful of air and then begin to slowly exhale, squeezing the trigger, cocking and squeezing again in rapid succession. The weapon made a cracking sound, somewhere between the crack of a bullwhip and the bang of a cherry bomb firecracker. Hal Burns and Janet Croft both probably heard the first shot, but only Janet could've heard the second. The first round entered the back of Hal's skull and out the front, taking a good bit of brain matter, bone, and blood with it, and pierced Janet just above her pubic mound. A few seconds later, faster than Janet's brain could've processed that, one, she'd been shot in the gut, and two, she was covered with matter from Hal's head, another round struck her right between the eyes. The projectile made a small little finger-sized hole in her face, and one the size of a small woman's fist coming out the back, spattering the lowered window with flesh, blood, bits of bone, and brain matter.

The man in black lowered his weapon and smiled.

"How thoughtful of them to lower the windows for me," he said to the wind and trees. "No glass to affect the trajectory."

He stepped closer and looked inside the gore-spattered interior of the car and was pleased with what he saw.

"Perfect," he said. "Just one small thing to do."

He whistled while he worked.

Charles Ray

CHAPTER 10

Greg and Meade drove into the parking lot behind the police department at the same time, Greg a few seconds ahead of his partner. They parked, greeted each other, and walked silently to their office, where, after getting their second morning cup of coffee, they sat at their desks and stared at the whiteboard upon which nothing new had been added since getting Dr. Stone's autopsy report.

"So, partner," Meade said. "What do we do today?"

That question had troubled Greg's sleep, but no useful answer had come to him.

"Damned if I know," he said. "I suppose we could go over to the school and see what we can dig up about the victims. See if there's anything in their backgrounds that might make someone want to kill them."

Meade stood and adjusted his jacket. "Reckon that beats sitting around here with our thumbs up our asses."

Just as Greg stood, Chief Hoag walked in. He had a constipated look on his florid face.

"Morning, chief,'" Greg said. "Larry and I were just going over to the school to see what we could find out about our two vics."

"Put that on hold, Greg," Hoag said, surprising Greg by using his first name for the first time. "We've got another two bodies. This time in Spark's Grove."

Greg looked confused. "That's a popular spot for people to park when they're too cheap to rent a motel room," Meade said. "Is it the same M.O. as our first two victims, chief?"

"I don't know. A patrol found 'em. The officer who called it in is a rookie, and he sounded on the radio like he was about to upchuck, so I figure it's pretty gruesome. You two take a look at it, and if . . . well, just let me know what you find."

Without waiting for a reply, he turned and left.

"Well," Greg said. "It beats doing a lot of interviews that would yield us zip. Let's roll."

Greg let Meade drive this time, since he knew exactly where he was going and it was quicker than Greg driving with Meade giving him turn directions a second or two before he had to make said turn. He sat back and mentally catalogued the landmarks they passed, all part of his 'getting to know' Darden. A driver with a heavy foot, Meade made the ten-mile trip in twelve minutes, breaking every speed limit on every street and road over which they traveled, but it also meant that Marcus Stone, for once, didn't beat them to a crime scene. He pulled up in his pearl-gray Cadillac a few seconds after they did.

The young patrol officer who'd found the bodies had gathered his wits sufficiently to string crime scene tape around the vehicle in a twenty-foot circle. He stood just outside the tape, still looking a bit sick. As he passed him, Greg complimented him on the initiative with the tape, but suggested he move it out another ten feet just on the off chance the perpetrator got sloppy and left some small piece of evidence as he departed the scene. Not that he expected that to happen, but he always believed in playing it safe.

Stone joined them just as Meade lifted the tape for them to go under it.

"Hey, doc," he said. "You must be pretty busy today. This is the first time I can remember we beat you to a scene."

"I had a patient in my office," Stone said. "And, my live patients take precedence over the dead ones."

He pushed past Meade, nodded at Greg, and made a beeline for the car sitting in the clearing. Even from ten feet away, Greg could see the spatter. The vehicle looked like an abattoir. He took out the tube of Bengay ™ and smeared some under his nose. He normally used it whenever called to a scene where the corpse had been cooking for a while, but he knew that this much blood would also generate a sickening odor. Meade watched him and then held out his hand.

"Didn't know your big city cops used things like this," he said. "Figured you got so many calls like this, you'd be used to it."

Greg shook his head. "Some things you never get used to."

By the time they arrived at the car, Stone had donned his white overalls and had his head stuck inside the driver-side window. While they waited, Greg visually surveyed the scene. The blood spatter was all inside, mostly on the passenger side, but a few scattered marks on the inside of the front window. Past Stone he could see the victims, a man and a woman, and, as Stone turned the man's head, he could see that most of the front of his head, down to the bridge of his nose, was missing.

"Holy shit," Meade said. "Looks like someone used a pretty large caliber round on that dude."

Greg shook his head, not in disagreement, but in disgust at what he was seeing.

"It's overkill for sure," he said. "Looks like the window on the driver's side was down, and the killer shot through it. I wonder how far away he was."

Stone pulled back out of the car and turned to face them. "Hell, he could've been right up next to the car, and I doubt these two would've noticed."

"Why's that, doc?" Meade asked.

Stone jerked his thumb at the car. "Take a look for yourself."

Greg and Meade peered in, and their eyes went wide.

"Holy shit," Meade said. "The dude's fly is open and his willie's hanging out . . . you mean—"

"Precisely," Stone said. "I figure they were *in flagrante delicto*, and thus, oblivious to whatever else was going on around them."

"You mean she was gobbling his knob?"

"Or, greasing the stick," Stone said.

"Okay, you two, grow up," Greg said, but he was unable to suppress a smile at their locker room banter. "So, they were having sex, and somebody came up on 'em and offed 'em, is that about it, doc?"

"Yeah, that's about it. I won't know officially until I complete an autopsy, but I think it's safe to say that cause of death is gunshot wounds, high caliber round fired from relatively close range."

"We'll also need their identities as soon as possible."

"Oh, I can give you that right now," Stone said. "I recognize the woman. She's the head teller at Mercantile Bank, where the hospital has its accounts. Name's Janet Croft. And, I'd recognize this Mercedes anywhere, with that vanity plate, Brn2Crz. It belongs to Hal Burns, president of Mercantile, and that gray expensive looking suit the male vic's wearing is just like one I've seen Hal wear on a number of occasions."

Greg pulled out his notebook and entered the information. "Is there anyone in this town you don't know, doc?"

"A few newcomers or teenagers, maybe. I've either delivered or treated nearly everyone in town at one time or another."

"Lucky for us. It'll at least save us the time trying to identify them and track down next of kin."

"I can help you there, too," Stone said. "Hal's wife, Myra, lives in Pinegrove Community, the gated housing area just north of town, and Janet's husband, Winston, will be at his store, Croft's Hardware, on Main Street."

Greg made more notes. "You sure about those IDs, doc? Wouldn't want to upset the wrong people with tragic news like this."

"One hundred percent. But, that's not your main problem with this one, my friend."

"Oh, what *is* our main problem then?"

"Did you take a look at the blood on the windshield?"

"Yeah," Greg said. "Not unusual to have a lot of blood splatter in gunshot cases."

Stone chuckled mirthlessly. "I think you'd better take a closer look, Greg, only from the inside."

Not really wanting to get any closer to the gory scene than he absolutely had to, Greg was reluctant to stick his head inside the car. But, something in Stone's voice told him it was important. He took a deep breath and leaned in through the open side window. When his eyes had adjusted to the slightly darker interior of the car, he focused on the spatter marks on the windshield, and felt an immediate lurch in the pit of his stomach.

Written in blood, the neatly done block letters had looked like random blood spatter from the outside, but from inside, they were crystal clear, and chilling.

Let the marriage bed be undefiled

He jerked back, bumping his head against the top of the door frame. "Shit, I don't believe it," he said.

"Believe it," Stone said.

"It's just like the letters carved into that girl's stomach."

"I'd say done by the same person."

Meade looked from Greg to Stone, a perplexed expression on his face. "What the fuck you two talkin' about?"

"Different weapon, same killer," Stone said.

"He left us another message," Greg said. "Since, the victims weren't married to each other and were cheating, I suppose that's what the message relates to."

"You think one of the spouses was involved?"

Greg knew that his partner was just being logical. In most homicides, a close relative, like a cheated-on or battered spouse, was the most likely perpetrator. But, he didn't think that applied in this case . . . these *two* cases.

"Ordinarily, that's the first place I'd look," he said. "But, if this is the same killer, and I think the doc's right, what's the connection between the first two victims and these two?"

"Uh, damn, hadn't thought about that. You ain't gonna get back on that serial killer hobby horse, are you?"

Greg stared hard at his partner. "No, I got that message loud and clear. You'll not hear me use that term, not even once. *But*, we're gonna have to investigate this as if it was a serial killer we're chasing. We can't rule out other suspects, the vic's husband for example, but I think that's a dead end. If this had been a spur of the moment passion killing, I don't think the killer would've taken the time afterwards to write a message. No, we've got a warped mind at work here, and that has to be our main effort."

Meade rubbed his chin. "Hell, what you say makes sense. About as much sense as anything about these cases. Okay, we'll do it your way. But, man, I hope you're wrong. A serial killer would ruin the tourist trade, and the mayor would never forgive us for it."

"You mean he'd never forgive *me* for it."

Meade shook his head. "Nah, partner. We're in this together. We share the prize, we share the pain."

Charles Ray

CHAPTER 11

After instructing two new uniforms who'd arrived on the scene to canvas the area to see if there might be any witnesses, they left Stone and the crime scene techs to process the scene and went back to police headquarters.

Greg briefed Chief Hoag on the new case, and beyond stating that they believed they were related, didn't press the issue. Back at their desks, they rearranged the whiteboard, adding Hal Burns and Janet Croft's names to it.

"You know," Meade said. "I don't think the patrol guys are gonna turn up anything. Not a lot of traffic on that road at night."

"I didn't think so either, but we have to cover all bases."

"So, what do we do now?"

Greg massaged the bridge of his nose. He was beginning to feel a migraine coming on. "While we wait for doc's post-mortem, let's try and put together some victim profiles. Maybe that'll have a hint that points us toward the killer."

Not a fan of the desk work that went along with being a detective, Meade frowned. "What good's that donna do us? I can't imagine a connection between two teens and two adults who worked in a bank and were bonking each other on the sly."

"From what the doc told us, though," Greg said. "The two teens were having sex when they were attacked. In fact, the similarity is that in both cases it appears to have been oral sex."

Meade's brows did a little wiggling dance.

"Whoa! You tryin' to tell me you think we got a killer who gets set off by people doing the old sixty-nine?"

"No, not really." Greg held his hands up in surrender. "I'm just brain storming. We know, for instance, that sex is a common thread between the two cases, so let's keep that in mind. In the meantime, let's see if we can find any other commonalities, no matter how remote."

"Yeah, yeah, I know you're right, but this is gonna mean some real hard thinking, and hard thinking's not my strong suit. I'm much better out on the streets."

Greg stood. "Okay, let's try doing a little thinking on our feet. We'll go first to the bank and talk to the people who work there. See if any of them know anything."

"All right, now that kind of detective work I don't mind."

The trip to the bank, which was located six blocks from police headquarters, yielded nothing of real value. Many of the people working there suspected that the owner and the head teller were having an affair, but fearful for their jobs, kept it to themselves. No one thought that either of their spouses knew about their dalliances but couldn't swear to it. None of them knew either spouse, so Greg decided their next order of business would be to swing by Stone's place and get a hundred percent confirmation on identity and then call on each spouse to deliver the sad news; and, at the same time, see if either of them acted guilty.

At the hospital, they were told that Stone was conducting an autopsy, not Greg's favorite activity, but he figured it would look good to the chief and the mayor if the doctor could tell them that he'd observed the autopsy, even if only for a few minutes.

They found him, dressed in bloody scrubs, up to his forearms in the open chest of Hal Burns. He kept working but looked over his shoulder at them.

"Well, if it isn't my favorite two detectives. Come to watch me work?"

Greg had never gotten inured to being casual around dead bodies. He took a quick glance at the corpse and then focused his gaze on Stone's face.

"You mind letting the chief know we did?" Stone nodded. The wrinkling of the mask over his face indicated that he smiled as well. "Look, we need to notify the next of kin, so I wanted to make sure of the IDs."

"ID is confirmed," Stone said. "This specimen you see before you is the late Hal Burns. Death caused by a single round that entered the back of his skull and blew out the front. The right-side window of the car was open, so the slug's out there in the woods somewhere. I finished Janet Croft's autopsy already, and yes, it was her. Same COD, single, high-velocity round to the forehead, took out the back of her head. She must have raised her head when Hal was hit. Round that killed her is also not present, so I can't tell you the exact caliber yet. Oh, and she had traces of semen in her mouth, so our initial assessment of what they were doing was correct."

"TMI, doc, too damn much information," Meade said. "Greg, can we get outa here? The smell of formaldehyde makes me want to puke."

Stone snorted and turned back to the corpse. Greg gave Meade a gentle push to hurry him out of the room. He didn't take a deep breath until they were outside in the parking lot.

"You should go easy on the doc, Larry," he said. "We don't want to alienate him."

"Aw, don't worry. Me 'n doc been bantering like that ever since I became a detective. 'Sides, he's kinda sweet on my mom, so that sort of makes him my almost step-father."

Greg scrunched his eyes shut, opened them, and looked at his partner in amazement. The town of Darden never ceased to amaze him. He let out a breath and shook his head.

"Okay, then," he said. "Which should we go first, the widow or the widower?"

"Pinegrove's closest to here. I say we do Mrs. Burns first."

Greg nodded. "You drive," he said. "I'm not sure I know where this place is."

"I've never been inside, but I've driven past it a few times. Let's go."

The drive to Pinegrove Community, a mid-sized collection of overpriced McMansions inhabited by most of Darden's wealthy set, was a few miles from the hospital, about fifty yards off the highway, surrounded by a six-foot high brick wall, with an electronically operated gate and a uniformed guard in a booth to screen everyone entering. Greg had seen gated communities before, but this one had tighter security than most. Apparently, the small-town coziness and sense of neighborliness ended at its wall.

The guard, after Meade flashed his badge, pressed a button, causing the steel bar to raise. Meade asked the man for directions to the Burns' house and was told that the Burns *residence* was the fifth house on the left up the street they were on.

"Can you believe that shit? They live in residences out here and not houses like the rest of us," he said to Greg as he drove. "What a bunch of pretenders."

This was a side of Meade that Greg hadn't seen before. He'd just assumed from the expensive suits he wore, and his easy manner with the police chief and Dr. Stone, that he was from a wealthy family. But, there was, apparently, another layer of wealth in Darden above his level, and little in the way of good feelings between them. He didn't respond to Meade's obviously—or so he hoped—question, but this was an aspect of his new home he needed to look into.

The house was huge, a red brick, two-story colonial with a circular driveway and a three-car garage. The lawn, larger than the police department parking lot by several multiples, was well-manicured and the flowers lining the driveway looked like they got lots of attention. Greg contrasted what he was seeing with the one-story Cape Cod he lived in on Darden's west side, with its postage-stamp-sized lawn and a few azalea plants that he never had time to water, much less prune.

Meade parked the Crown Vic in front of one of the three doors of the garage, and they got out.

"So, this is how the other half lives," Greg said. "Not too shabby."

"Not half, my friend," Meade said. "They're less than five percent of the town's population, but among them, they control over eighty percent of the wealth."

"A good job if you can get it."

Meade didn't respond. At the door, Greg pressed the brass button set into a black marble frame at the side. He could hear a classical tune playing somewhere deep inside the house.

In a few seconds, while the echo of the doorbell was still sounding, the door opened, and he took an involuntary step back.

The woman in a black dress with white cuffs and collar didn't seem to notice. Greg fought to keep his face impassive as he looked down at the most unusual sight he'd seen since coming to Darden, the crime scenes excepted. She wasn't much more than an inch over five feet tall, with a head that was too big for her body. The white cap she wore barely contained the stringy white hair that hung down on the sides and back of her head. But, the thing that caught his eye was the fact that she was so wrinkled. He'd seen old people, and wrinkles didn't usually attract his attention, but this woman's face, arms and legs were *really* wrinkled. She looked like an inflatable rubber doll that someone had squeezed the air out of.

"What do ya want?" she asked. Her attitude matched her appearance.

"We'd like to speak with Mrs. Burns," he said.

"She expectin' ya?"

"No."

"Well, Missus Burns don't see no one without they got an appointment."

Greg pulled out his badge and held it in front of her nose. "This is official police business," he said. "It's important that we talk to her, so tell her that we're here, and be quick about it."

If he thought his tone would intimidate her, the expression of disdain she gave him would've put that to rest.

"Wait here," she said. "I'll tell her."

She stepped aside to let them enter, but her body language told them that the vestibule was as far as they were to go until further notice.

She was back in a few minutes, still with the sour look on her wrinkled face.

"The missus will see you in the sun room. Follow me."

She spun on her heels and marched, stiff-backed, through a living room filled with expensive-looking furniture that Greg couldn't have identified if his life depended on it, with oriental vases on little mahogany stands scattered about, and original oils and watercolors on the walls, through a sliding floor-to-ceiling glass door into a room that was almost as large as the entire ground floor of his house. The room had a large glass wall with a view of a manicured back yard filled with ornamental bushes and trees, and strategically placed beds of roses, in red, pink, yellow and white. The furniture was wicker that managed to still look opulent.

Lillian Burns, a slender woman of about fifty, dressed in a blue silk dressing gown that was open at the neck displaying her sun-freckled cleavage, sat on a wicker chair. At her elbow, on a wicker table, was a silver teapot, silver sugar and cream containers, and a delicate china cup containing a light brown liquid. She had icy blue eyes in an oval face that was porcelain smooth, and light brown, almost blonde, hair, swept back from her high forehead and arranged in a neat bun at the back of her head. She regarded Greg and Meade as if they were puppies who weren't allowed inside the house.

Greg took out his badge and held it up. "Mrs. Burns, I'm Detective Gregory Kildare, and this is Detective Larry Meade," he said. "Thank you for agreeing to speak with us."

"Abigail said you insisted," she said, waving a hand lazily at the maid who still lurked in the doorway. At the dismissal, she moved quietly away, but not before shooting a glare at Greg. "What is it you wish to discuss?"

"I'm afraid we have some bad news. Your husband, Hal Burns has been killed. I'm so sorry for your loss, but we need to ask you a few questions."

If he expected her to show some emotion after his announcement, he was to be disappointed. Her glacial look didn't change a bit.

"Hal's been killed? How?" Her tone of voice was no different than if she'd asked him what time it was.

"He was shot, ma'am."

"Do you know who did it?"

Greg shook his head. "No, but we're investigating it. Do you know of anyone who might want to harm your husband?"

She smiled, a cold, calculating smile that made Greg glad he didn't have to deal with her on a regular basis.

"Other than the husbands of the floozies he sleeps, uh slept, around with, no. Among his golfing colleagues he was really quite popular because he liked to bet on the game but is a lousy player."

"Your husband . . . slept around?" Not usually easy to shock, Greg was astounded at how cool she sounded when she said it.

"I suppose *slept around* is the euphemistic way to put it. To put it in terms that you might understand, detective, my husband screwed anything in a skirt every chance he got, married or single, it didn't matter to him."

"Didn't that upset you?"

"Why should it? If he was getting it elsewhere it meant he wouldn't be coming home to pester me. And, just in case you're thinking I might be a woman scorned, look around you. I get all this and don't even have to, how do they say it, put out for it. Now, of course, thanks to the inheritance laws of the state of Maryland, and the fact that Hal was nice enough to leave everything to me in his will, it's all mine." She smiled again. "But, if you're wondering why I'm not more stricken at the news of his demise, well, let's just say that our marriage was one of convenience from the start. We each gave the other what was wanted, for my part, financial security, for him, respectability. Now, will there be anything else?"

"Uh, no ma'am, I suppose not," Greg said. "If we have any further questions, we'll call and make an appointment."

"Yes, you do that. You can show yourselves out, I presume?"

She picked up the expensive cup and sipped delicately from it, dismissing them from her mind before they'd even gone. Greg and Meade looked at each other and shrugged in unison. Without a word, they turned and left, retracing their steps through the house.

Outside, as they were getting into the car, Meade looked over the roof at Greg. "That was one *coldhearted* woman."

"That she was," Greg said. "But, I don't think she's a viable suspect. She's not sad her husband's dead, but I don't think she's the type to dirty her hands or reputation on anything as sordid as murder."

"Yeah." Meade chuckled. "That would be too lower class. So, we off to see the husband of the other vic?"

"Yeah, let's roll."

Croft's store, a sprawling one-story concrete block building with parking lots on both sides, occupied a complete city block not more than ten minutes from police headquarters. Meade pulled into an empty parking space near the entrance, and the two of them entered the store.

A pimply-faced teenager with spiked red hair, wearing a neon blue shirt, met them at the door. "Welcome to Crofts. Can I be of service?"

"Yeah, we'd like to talk to the owner," Greg said, flashing his badge.

The boy's eyes got as round as saucers as he stared at the badge.

"Well, don't just stand there," Meade said. "Go get Mr. Croft. Chop, chop."

"Uh, yessir, right away sir," the kid said. He spun and ran toward the back of the store, zig-zagging through the shelves that were stacked with tools, guns, fishing gear, tents, and just about everything, Greg thought, that the manly-man needed to buttress his manhood.

After a few minutes, the kid came back, followed by a muscular, gray-haired man of middle height, with a confused look on his face.

"What can I do for you, officers?" he asked.

"Mr. Croft, I'm Detective Kildare, and this is Detective Meade. Is there somewhere we can talk private?"

"Sure, we can talk in my office. Follow me."

Croft turned and headed back the way he'd come, with Greg and Meade in tow, staying close to avoid getting lost in the expanse of shelves, some reaching to the ceiling, and all so heavily stocked it was impossible to see who was in the next aisle.

They went through a large roll-up door, through a warehouse, and down a short hallway to the back of the building. Croft's office was small, a bit larger than the space Greg and Meade shared at headquarters, and his desk was piled high with papers. Boxes of papers were stacked behind the desk. Two wooden chairs were in front, and a scuffed leather executive chair was behind the desk. Croft motioned at the wooden chairs and plopped down in the leather chair. It made a loud squeaking sound as his body settled in.

"Okay, gentlemen, what can I do for you?"

"Mr. Croft," Greg said. "I'm afraid I have some bad news about your wife."

"Janet? What about her? She in an accident or something?"

Greg hesitated a few seconds, watching the man. His reaction of shock seemed legitimate. How he reacted to what Greg said next would be telling.

"No, sir, I'm afraid not," he said. "Your wife was shot. I'm so sorry to have to tell you this, but she's . . . dead."

Croft's face went pale. Tears welled up in his eyes. "Dead? Shot? W-what do you mean? How could . . . who would shoot Janet? Was it a robbery?"

Unless he was a damn good actor, the tears were real, and the shock on his face, the pain, seemed real.

"No, Mr. Croft, it wasn't a robbery. Your wife was at . . ." He turned to Meade.

"Your wife was in Spark's Grove, Mr. Croft," Meade said.

Croft's face went from pale to red. "Spark's Grove? What the hell was she doing there? When did this happen?"

"The M.E. hasn't established time of death yet, sir," Greg said. "But, we think it was sometime before midnight last night."

Croft clenched his eyes shut and shook his head. When he opened his eyes, Greg could see understanding dawning in them.

"She wasn't there alone, was she?"

"No, I'm afraid not."

"Who was she with?"

"The other victim is, was, Hal Burns. Do you know him?"

"Yeah, I know that son of a bitch. He's Janet's boss. He's got a reputation as a skirt chaser. I'd always heard he liked 'em young, though." He massaged his eye sockets with the knuckles of both hands. "Well, that explains Janet gettin' promoted to head teller after only six years at the bank."

"You didn't suspect your wife was . . ."

"Fuckin' her boss? No, I didn't. Oh, I ain't no fool, and I know I spend too much time in this damn store, so it wouldn't surprise me to know she was gettin' a little on the side. But, her boss. T-that's, that's . . . oh, hell, I . . . I left the house early yesterday, and slept in the office last night, 'cause we worked so late doin' inventory."

He dropped his face into his cupped hands and began weeping openly, his body shaking.

Greg and Meade stood.

"Look, Mr. Croft, we can come back and do this another time," Greg said. "I'm truly sorry for your loss."

Croft raised his head and wiped his eyes. "No, that's okay. Go ahead and ask your questions."

"Can you think of anyone who would want to hurt your wife?"

It was a standard question to which Greg already knew the answer, the same answer that every family member gave when told that someone close to them has been killed—everyone loved her.

"No, I don't. Everyone loved Janet."

"I would imagine when she got promoted at the bank, and from what you just said, probably ahead of more senior employees, there would've been hard feelings."

Croft laughed bitterly. "Of course, there were some hard feelings. Haven't you ever been pissed when someone got promoted when you felt it should've been you? But, mad enough to kill her? No way."

Greg could understand that, not from his own experience, but he'd seen the hard looks he'd gotten occasionally around the Darden Police Department, him, the outsider, coming in and taking a job that should've gone to a local. But, Croft was right. Such feelings hardly ever rose to that degree."

"How about Burns? Is it possible someone had it in for him, and she was just in the wrong place at the wrong time?"

"That bank Burns runs holds mortgages on just about every business in town, and a good number of houses around the area. I suppose somebody could be pissed about owin' him so much, but again, I don't see anybody in this town goin' that far. This is a small town, and just about everybody knows everybody else. Except for the occasional husband-wife spat that gets out of control, we've almost never had any violence here. Hell, I don't remember the last somebody actually got killed. Maybe back when I was in high school, but I'm not even sure about that."

Greg noticed that Croft's eyes were dry now, and he seemed to have his emotions under control. He could think of no more questions to ask him. He'd already sort of answered the standard 'where were you around the time of the incident' question, and Greg would check that out.

"Thank you for your time," he said. "If we have any more questions, we'll get in touch."

"When can I get my wife's body? I need to make funeral arrangements."

"That'll be up to Dr. Stone. I'm sure he'll release it as soon as he's completed his examination. He'll probably be in touch with you for an official identification; you can ask him then."

"Thank you, detective . . . Kildare, was it? You're the new man in town."

"Yeah, guess you could say that. I've been here three weeks."

"Some welcome to Darden, eh? Where'd you work before?"

"I was with the police force in DC."

Croft nodded. "Well then, I guess you're used to dealing with murder cases."

Greg bristled inside at the assumption people always made about the District of Columbia. Yes, the murder rate was high, but no higher than any other major metropolitan area, and a lot lower than most cities its size. But, he remembered that he was in a small town now, and one of his jobs would be to get along with the locals.

"Yeah, I've done one or two. Again, Mr. Croft, I'm sorry for your loss. We'll be in touch." Croft stood. "That's okay, we'll see ourselves out."

He sat back down and cradled his head in his hands again.

Outside in the parking lot, Greg put a hand on his partner's shoulder before they got into the car.

"What'd you make of him, Larry? You think he's a viable suspect?"

"I don't know, man. I don't know him all that well. He graduated from high school about eight years ahead of me. I remember he was on the football team is all. I've never known him to get into any trouble. He took over the hardware store from his old man when he died; the same year him and Janet got married. And, he did seem pretty broken up."

"Yeah. He was either genuinely shocked or he's a damn good actor. But, I tend to agree with you. He's not our man. Still, though, we'll keep him on our radar, just to be on the safe side. You see all those guns in there? Hell, he could've used one of the guns he's got in stock. Unless the doc can identify a specific weapon, it'd take weeks, if not months, to test everyone of 'em."

'What I hear you sayin', partner, is that we're back to square one. Neither spouse seems good for this one, so that leaves us with a completely unknown killer out there somewhere."

"The worse kind of case," Greg said, shaking his head. "No known motive, and no suspect. Partner, we're flying blind on this one."

CHAPTER 12

Greg still had the cases on his mind when he got home that evening. He put a pan of water on the stove and took out a package of ramen noodles from the cupboard. Then, he opened a can of Coors and sipped from it while he waited for the water to boil.

He had another beer with the noodles and then took a third can and went into his tiny living room, turned the TV on and sat idly watching the evening news on CNN, while his mind still roiled.

Finally, he decided that he needed a real professional opinion, and to hell with Hoag's prohibition against involving any other police agency in the case. Of course, what he planned wasn't exactly official, but he couldn't think of anything else to do.

He pulled out his phone and dialed a number he hadn't called in over a year.

The phone rang three times before a voice that was seared into his memory answered.

"Hello, stranger, it's been a long time since you called me. What's up?"

"Hey, Alison, this is Greg, Greg Kildare," he said.

"I know that, silly. Haven't you ever heard of Caller ID? I have you in my phone even though you haven't called me in fourteen months."

"Damn, has it been that long? I'm sorry, but I've been going through a lot of shit, and the time just got away from me. You got time to talk?"

"For you, Greg, there's always time. After all, you were my favorite student."

Two years previously, Greg had been chosen to attend the FBI's profiling training in Quantico, Virginia, a class taught by Alison Holloway, the FBI's top profiler. He'd been thrilled at being selected, and when he discovered that the instructor was a drop-dead gorgeous, petite woman with shiny brown hair she wore in an old-fashioned page boy cut, he'd paid extra attention in class. Along with getting an eyeful every day, he'd also learned a lot. For one thing, he'd learned that instructors at the academy didn't have rules against romantic relationships with students from outside the FBI, and during the six-week program, which was part of the Violent Criminal Apprehension Program, or VICAP, they spent many evenings rumpling the sheets in her bedroom in the small frame house she lived in just of U.S. Route 1, south of the Quantico Marine Corps Base where the FBI Academy was housed. They'd made no commitments to each other, but after completing the program, he'd driven down a couple of weekends and they'd gone once to Colonial Williamsburg for a long weekend. But, when he was moved to the serial crimes unit in DC, his workload increased to a point where personal relationships had to take a backseat, and he'd stopped visiting, and had eventually stopped calling, thinking that long-distance relationships were just too hard to maintain.

"Look, Alison, first, I'm sorry I cut you off like I did," he said. "I was goin' through a lot of stuff, and my mind was all messed up. I hope we can still be friends."

There was a long pause, and he feared she'd hung up.

Then, she spoke. "I understand, really I do. And, I have this feeling, that your call now is not just to get back in touch. You have a problem, and you need my help."

"Damn, girl, do you do mind reading as well as profiling?"

"No, but I can sense the tension in your voice even over the phone, and it has nothing to do with our . . . relationship."

"You're good, really good. That's why I called you." He then explained the two cases to her, leaving out nothing.

"I don't have much to go on," she said when he'd finished. "But, my rough assessment is that you *and* your chief are wrong."

"Wha-, whaddya mean we're *both* wrong?"

"Remember my lecture? A serial killer is someone who kills three or more people, usually to satisfy some warped psychological itch—"

"We have that, Alison," he said, cutting her off. "This guy's killed four people."

"Let me finish, grasshopper," she said in a poor imitation of the 'Karate Kid' character. "These killings usually take place over more than a month, with a cooling off period between murders. Now, our official bureau definition is a series of two or more murders, committed as separate events by a person acting alone in most, but not all, cases. Now, what you have here are four corpses, but only two events, and with hardly any down time between events, right?"

"Yeah, so?"

"What you have here is what we call a spree killer; someone who kills multiple victims in multiple locations with little or no time between murders."

"Oh, I see. So, what's the difference as far as catching this son of a bitch is concerned?"

"Predictability, Greg. Remember what I taught you. A serial killer, unless he or she makes a mistake, will go on indefinitely. A spree killer, though, is a different kettle of fish. Something happened to trigger the spree. When the impact of the trigger wans, he'll go dormant. Unless you can figure out what set him off, or get some kind of forensic evidence to point in his direction, he'll just fade away."

"Holy shit. The mayor's gonna have a conniption fit if he gets wind of this."

"If this is a spree killer, your mayor's likely to have that fit sooner rather than later. You know, you could use the bureau's resources on this."

"Ain't gonna happen. The mayor's against the negative publicity involving the feds would generate, and the police chief just doesn't like working with other agencies—or, that's how I see it. So, I need you to keep this call between the two of us. If it got out that I reached out to you, my ass could be on the street."

"The bureau only comes in when invited, and this hasn't crossed state lines, so no problem keeping it between us. You know, of course, you can call me anytime, and not necessarily about this case."

He clenched the phone, thinking about so many lost opportunities. Was there a chance to redeem himself?

"I, I'd like that, Alison. Now that I'm working in a small town, I might even be able to get some time off to come down to see you, that is, if you're okay with that."

"I'm more than okay with it, you ninny. Jeesh, you're slow on the uptake, and you were such a bright student."

He let out a breath. This was the Alison he remembered, always quick with a quip, and to forgive human frailty.

"Say, I have an idea," he said. "Darden's right on the Chesapeake. Some beautiful views, and charter boat rides. I think you'd love it. Maybe you could come up here when you get some time off."

"Sounds like a plan. Right now, with you up to your neck in a murder investigation, is probably not a good time. But, as soon as things clear up I think I'd like to visit."

Murder case be damned, he was suddenly feeling good.

"You don't know how good it makes me feel to hear you say that, Alison."

She chuckled. "Probably as good as hearing your voice made me feel."

They chatted for a few more minutes, and then, after he promised that he'd call more often, and not just to pick her brain about business, he hung up. His dour mood was gone. Suddenly, anything seemed possible.

Charles Ray

CHAPTER 13

The following morning, Greg and Meade found themselves where they were after the first murders, sitting at their desks staring at the whiteboard that, except for the names of the victims and the estimated times and causes of deaths, was bare.

"This case is beginning to get to me," Meade said. "I hardly got a wink of sleep last night thinking about it."

Greg smiled. "I slept like a log."

Meade looked at him for a long moment. "Did you get laid or take sleeping pills?"

Despite his swarthy complexion, thanks to the combination of African, Native American, and Mediterranean ancestry, Greg was fully capable of blushing darkly. He felt his cheeks getting warm.

"Uh, no, I just came to terms with this case," he said.

Meade grinned and pointed a finger at him. "You got laid. I know the signs, even though it's been a while for me. Who is it? Yvette from the diner? Or, that cute Indian nurse out at Doc Stone's hospital? You dog, you. Been in town less than a month, and already you get lucky. What's your secret?"

Greg flapped his hands.

"No, it's not like that, really. I barely know Yvette Landau, and she's never given me the time of day, other than to take my lunch order. As for the nurse, I don't even know her name."

"It's Vana Siharda, just in case you're interested. And, as for Yvette, you might not have noticed, but I've seen her giving you the eye more than once. She's hot for that bod of yours, partner, take my word for it."

If Alison hadn't come back into his life, even if only over the phone, he might have been interested, but for now, he wanted to give their relationship a chance. Not that he was a one-woman man by any means, but there was something about Alison Holloway that made him want to be.

"Look, let's focus on the case. Last night before I went to bed I had an epiphany, one of those eureka moments." He wasn't quite ready to tell Meade about Alison. "I realized that you and the chief are right, we don't have a serial killer on our hands."

"Well, it's wise of you to see it that way, partner," Meade said. "Although, after yesterday's case, I was beginning to think you were on to something. So, we have a vicious, probable male, who gets off on killing couples. What do we call him, the Valentine Killer, the Buzz Killer? Naw, that last one would only work if he used a power saw as a murder weapon."

Despite himself, Greg laughed. "I definitely *don't* want to give this turkey a name. That'd be sure to hit the media, and it'd just encourage and embolden him. No, for now, he's just an unknown individual wanted in connection with four homicides, a person of interest. And, there will be no mention of a serial killer, because what he is . . . our perp is a spree killer."

Meade's eyes went wide and he sat back in his chair as if he'd been punched in the chest.

"Spree, you're kidding, right," he said in a choked voice. "You think telling Chief Hoag we got a spree killer running around Darden getting his jollies by offing people is gonna make him happy? Hell, Greg, the man will have a massive coronary, right after he fires your ass."

"Didn't say we were gonna tell the chief. But, I felt it important that you know what we're dealing with.

Whoever this perp is, he's likely to strike again. You might have something in this thing about him going after couples. We need to flesh out some kind of profile that might help us predict where he might strike next."

"Man, that's a tall order. I don't know if we have the skill to do that."

Greg smiled. "Well, amigo, you're in luck. It just so happens that I got the chance to attend the FBI's class on profiling a while back, and I still remember most of what they taught me. I think I can get a picture of this dude with a little more information. It'd help if we had more than the old guy's weak description of the man he saw in the park. I know this is a small town, but that's all the more reason someone should've seen something."

"Yeah, I know what you mean, but the park and that cove where Burns and Janet Croft were killed aren't that close to where people live. There's no real place from where you can see—wait a minute, there is one place from where you can see both scenes. I don't know why I hadn't thought about it before."

"Really?" Greg said, looking surprised. "In this town, there's a place that has a view of both murder scenes?"

"Yeah, but you're not gonna like it when I tell you where."

"Why is that?"

"It's the Caldecott Mansion on that little bluff overlooking the bay. From there, you can see the whole damn town."

For some reason the name Caldecott rang a bell with Greg, but he couldn't remember where he'd heard it before.

"Why should that bother me?"

"Aw, come on, you mean you bean here almost a month, and you don't know the story of the Caldecott family?"

"I suppose not. Enlighten me."

"Well, rumor is this town was founded in 1804 by two families, the Dardens and the Caldecotts. Back then the Dardens were the most powerful, so they got to name the town, thus, it's Darden. The Caldecotts never forgave them for it. They say old man Chester Darden, that's the one from back in the 1800s, became a multimillionaire just to spite the Dardens. He built that big house on that bluff so his ancestors could look down on the Dardens and everyone else in town for eternity. Some folks think his ghost hangs around up there."

"Hey, maybe we can ask the ghost if he saw anything." Greg stood. "Let's go talk to folks at the Caldecott Mansion."

"They don't like visitors up there."

"We're not visitors. This is official police business. Let's roll."

CHAPTER 14

Greg hadn't given any thought to Caldecott Mansion, thinking that rich people had an annoying tendency to bestow fancy names on things as a way to highlight their status, so he was totally unprepared for his first glimpse of the place.

It sat at the top of a bluff overlooking Chesapeake Bay, at the end of a mile-long serpentine gravel road that was lined by stately oaks and elms on both sides, obscuring the view of the structure until one made that last hairpin turn in the road.

And, when they did, what came into Greg's view, reminded him of the house of the Munster family in the TV comedy show about a family of ghouls living cheek by jowl with ordinary people. It was three stories high, or four if you counted the towers with their bell-shaped roofs at the front and rear.

Constructed of dark gray stone, with the morning sun behind it, the house had an ominous mien, and with gable roofs on the north end and mansard roofs with large dormer windows on the south, it looked like either the architect or the builder couldn't make up his mind what style he wanted. The surface of the roofs was large slates, the same color of the stone of the walls. In the front center was a large porte-cochere, the roof of which reached the sills of the second=floor windows, with archways high enough to accommodate a hansom cab with a top-hatted driver.

"Jesus," he said. "This place is creepy. I'd sure hate to have to come up here at night."

"What I hear, you wouldn't be welcome," Meade said. "Matter of fact, I doubt they'll welcome us this morning."

"These Caldecotts don't sound too friendly."

"There's only one now. Maxmillian the third, and yeah, he spells his name without the third 'I', so don't forget to pronounce it without it. I hear he can be a bit picky about that. Anyway, his old man died a few years back, and Max was his sole heir."

'Wasn't there a Mrs. Caldecott?"

"Yeah, there is, or was. No one's sure. She hasn't been seen in over ten years. Rumor floated around that she ran off with the gardener. Anyway, except for the household and ground staff, there's just Maxmillian."

Meade pulled the Crown Vic under the porte-cochere and killed the engine. He sat there with his hands resting on the steering wheel, staring straight ahead.

"What's the matter? Why're we waiting?" Greg asked.

Meade shook himself. "I don't know, man. I was raised in this town, and this is the first time in my life I've been up here. This whole hill's off limits to townsfolk. It's one of the few places even teenagers avoid."

"What? It's haunted?"

"Nah, nothin' like that. It's just that the Caldecotts valued their privacy, and threatened legal action to anyone who trespassed. So, no one ever trespassed."

"Well, partner, we're not trespassing. We're here on police business, so let's get cracking."

Greg unfastened his seat belt and slid out of the car. He heard the thunk of the door as Meade exited the driver's side. Standing there, he looked up at the wide double doors with their stained-glass windows set at eye-level. The place was quiet. As quiet as a graveyard, he thought.

When Meade appeared at his side, he mounted the gray marble steps and pressed the brass button set into the door frame. He didn't hear the sound of a bell, assuming it was located somewhere deep inside the cavernous house. While they waited, he glanced around. He could see the top floors of the tallest buildings in Darden over the tops of the trees that flowed out from the base of the bluff, and had a clear view of the entrance to Raleigh Park. Looking the other way, he couldn't be sure he was looking at the second crime scene, but was pretty sure that site was also visible, especially from the upper floors of the house.

"You were right," he said to Meade. "From up here, you can look down on everyone in Darden."

"Uh," was all Meade said in reply.

He looked uncomfortable, but just as Greg was about to say something to ease his mind, one of the double doors swung inward.

After his reaction to the house, Greg expected to see a giant, pale version of the Munster's butler at the door. Instead, a gray-haired man about Greg's height, with a Roman nose and icy blue eyes, wearing what looked to Greg like an old-fashioned tuxedo, stood there, regarding them with an expression of barely concealed disdain."

"Yes," he said in an English accent. "May I help you, gentlemen?"

"We're here to talk to the owner of the house," Greg said. He took out his badge and held it up for the man to see.

"What do you wish to see Mr. Caldecott about?"

"I'd rather discuss that with him if you don't mind. It's official police business."

Greg used the tone he'd been taught in the academy. Not too forceful, but definitely not a request.

The butler made a sniffing noise through his nose. "Very well," he said after a pause. "You may wait here in the vestibule. I will see if Mr. Caldecott wishes to speak with you."

When the man had marched, stiff-backed, away. Meade nudged Greg in the side. "What are we gonna do if he refuses to talk to us?"

Greg shrugged. "Nothing we can do. He doesn't *have-* to talk to us. If he refuses, we leave."

They didn't have to leave. The butler returned, a sour look on his face, and told them that Caldecott would see them in the sun room. He then led them from the vestibule, through an immense room with high vaulted ceiling, lined with shadowy alcoves in which suits of armor stood like ancient, silent guards. Between the alcoves, ancient battle weapons hung on the walls. Their footsteps echoed off the walls as they crossed the cavernous space.

"Damn," Meade whispered. "It's like a museum in here. This stuff must be worth a small fortune."

"Try a large fortune," Greg said. "Some of those weapons on the walls are worth a few million on the antique market."

"How do you know that?""

"I worked the case of a murdered antique dealer back in DC. He dealt in stuff like this."

"So, this stuff's worth a few million? Wow!"

"No, partner, I mean, *one* of these things would probably fetch a few million, and that's on the legal market. On the black market, the sky's the limit."

Meade whistled, which drew a glare from the butler. Who, unlike them, didn't seem to make a sound as he glided across the floor.

"I don't think Jeeves likes me," Meade said.

Greg laughed, which drew another stare from the butler, who'd stopped at a pair of high double doors.

"The sun room is through here . . . gentlemen," he said. He swept the doors open, bowed slightly at the waist, and stepped aside.

They entered a room that was as bright as the room through which they'd just walked was gloomy. It was also the size of a regulation basketball court. Like a half-hexagon, it was nearly a hundred feet from side to side, and at least fifty feet from the entrance to the big glass wall that reached from the floor up twenty feet to the ceiling. The windowed wall had side panels, each about ten feet wide, giving a panoramic view, not only of the Chesapeake, but well back from the shoreline. The right wall had floor to ceiling bookshelves filled with leather-bound volumes, and the left wall had glass-front cases containing hunting rifles, pistols, knives, spears, bayonets, and shields—a veritable armory. In among the weaponry were black and white and color photos of men dressed in safari gear posing with dead animals. The room was otherwise sparsely furnished, with teak chairs and tables arranged so that those sitting could see the view through the wall.

A tall man, wearing a maroon smoking jacket and holding a large black pipe from which blue smoke drifted, stood beside one of the chairs watching Greg and Meade as they crossed the room, their shoes making clicking sounds on the polished wood floors. He was about Greg's height, and maybe a few pounds lighter, with the tanned complexion of someone who spends a lot of time outdoors. His dark brown hair, flecked with hints of gray, was combed straight back on an oval head, and his eyes, though brown, had a cold look in them.

When they drew near him, Greg took out his badge and held it up.

"Thanks for agreeing to see us, Mr. Caldecott," he said. "I'm Detective Greg Kildare, and this is my partner, Detective Larry Meade."

"You're welcome to my home, gentlemen," Caldecott said in a deep voice, with the slightest trace of an English accent. "Please, have a seat." He waved at two chairs on the other side of the teak table upon which sat a silver teapot. Next to the teapot was a thick, black leather-bound book, the title of which was so eroded, Greg couldn't read it. "Can I offer you a spot of tea?"

"No, thank you, sir, we're fine," Greg said.

As he and Meade sat, Caldecott remained standing. "How may I help you, gentlemen?"

"I assume, sir, that you're aware of the recent murders in Darden?"

Caldecott sat, crossed his legs and smoothed the legs of his trousers before responding. "My driver mentioned something about it, I believe," he said. "I'm afraid I don't concern myself much with the affairs of Darden, officer. Why do you wish to talk to me about it?"

"It's detective, sir. And, it just happens that from your property there's a clear view of both crime scenes, so we were wondering if you, or any of your staff might've seen anything that might help us."

Caldecott's left eyebrow arched upwards. Greg thought he was sneering at them, and that only added to the impression.

"I see. And, just when did these unfortunate incidents occur?"

Greg described the murders, focusing on the dates, time, and general locations, but left out the physical details of the crimes themselves or the statement of the old man in the park.

"I hardly think, detective, that one of my staff would witness a murder being committed and fail to report it," Caldecott said with a disdainful tone.

"I'm not suggesting that, sir. I merely think that with the vantage point you have up here, it's possible that from the upper floors of the house or the grounds, someone might have noticed something at either scene that might help us find whoever is responsible."

"I see. That, too is hardly likely, but if you wish to waste your time, I will allow you to talk to my staff. I'll have Henry assemble them."

He picked up a silver bell from behind the teapot and rang it.

Greg had to stifle a laugh when the butler appeared moments later and said, "You rang, sir?" in that posh English accent.

"Yes, Henry," Caldecott said. "Please assemble the staff in the parlor. These policemen would like to ask them some questions."

The butler bowed slightly at the waist. "As you wish, sir."

"There you are, gentlemen. Enjoy yourselves."

"What about you, sir? Did you see anything on the nights in question?" Greg asked.

"No, I did not. I do not spend my time looking down at that town. That was my great-grandfather, grandfather, and father's obsession, not mine, I assure you."

"Well, thank you for your cooperation anyway. I assume the parlor is the room we came through to get here?" Caldecott nodded stiffly. "We'll wait there for your staff."

Caldecott ignored him, sipping at his tea, acting as if he and Meade had already left the room.

Quietly, they rose and quickly crossed the room and left. Outside the sunroom, Meade leaned against the closed door. He wiped his forehead.

"Is it me, or did that dude give you the creeps, too?" Greg nodded.

"He ain't exactly Mr. Sunshine, that's for sure. I've met rich people before, and many of them tend to be aloof, sort of holier-than-thou, but this guy's the worst I've ever seen. He must be *really* rich."

"Oh, he is," Meade said. "Nobody knows exactly how much the Caldecott fortune's worth. They, well him now that his old man's dead, own over half the property around Darden, but nobody but his lawyer knows how much, or what else he owns. All I know is Maxmillian Caldecott the Third has never had to work a day in his life."

"I wonder what he does when he's not cooped up in this mausoleum,' Greg said.

"I hear he's a big game hunter like his dad. Always jetting off to some exotic place to bag some exotic animal."

"A trophy hunter? I saw the photos of hunting parties up there with the weapons, but I didn't see any trophies."

"Rumor is he keeps them in another room. Hell, that damn place must have a hundred rooms. Can you imagine having to execute a search warrant there?"

"I don't even want to think about that." Gregg shuddered.

They didn't have to wait long. Henry, the butler, who insisted on being called a 'gentleman's gentleman,' brought them in and ensconced them in a far corner so they could be brought forward one at a time. He, of course, was first, and set the tone for the interviews to follow.

When Greg asked him if he'd noticed anything at either of the two crime scenes on the nights and estimated times of the incidents, Henry tilted his head, regarding him down the length of his nose.

"Sir, as the manager of this household, I have better things to do than peer out the window at the goings on in the village below."

"I take that to mean you saw nothing," Greg said, making a note on his pad.

"That is correct."

"Okay, send the next person along."

The next person was Harriet, the maid, a geriatric wisp of a woman with iron-gray hair who didn't look robust enough to push a broom, much less take care of the cleaning of a place as huge as Caldecott

Mansion. She, of course, was too busy with her cleaning chores to notice anything outside the mansion. The groomsman slash driver, a cadaverous looking man with a high forehead and cold blue eyes, who reminded Greg of the butler in 'The Addams Family' TV show, said that it was after his normal work hours, and he was in his little chalet on the grounds of the mansion watching 'Fox News'.

Greg thanked them all for their time and dismissed them.

"Well, that was a total waste of time," Meade said.

"Yeah, but we have to check all the blocks. Let's get back to headquarters and decide our next move."

Charles Ray

CHAPTER 15

John Willis and Colin Nelson had been in love with each other since Willis had been the star quarterback on the Darden high school football team and Nelson had been his favorite wide receiver. Willis realized soon after Nelson joined the team that it was more than the wiry freshman's uncanny ability to catch a ball, no matter how poorly thrown, that attracted him. In the staunchly-conservative, evangelical-oriented Darden of their teens, though, they'd restricted their relationship to the occasional furtive groping in Raleigh Park or one of the two lover's hideaways along the bay coastline. After high school, Willis had gone to work for the local Winn-Dixie, eventually becoming manager, and Nelson went to work as a junior teller at Mercantile Bank. Being single, and high school classmates to boot, it wasn't unusual for them to room together. They shared a small A-frame house just south of town in a middle-class neighborhood, where they could do what they willed as long as they kept the curtains drawn.

Occasionally, though, they liked to visit Raleigh Park in the middle of the week late at night to recapture the old times. They picked mid-week and the late hour because the park wasn't frequented by many people at that time. No one knew about them, but now that the rest of the country was becoming more accepting of people with alternate life styles and sexual preferences, they were considering 'coming out.'

On this particular night, they had two reasons for the visit to Raleigh Park. One reason was to do a bit of nostalgic groping, but the more important reason was to discuss the impact of the momentous decision they were about to make.

Nelson, always the more practical of the two, insisted that they get that discussion out of the way so that it wouldn't be hanging like a shadow over their lovemaking, and Willis, as usual, agreed.

They sat, shoulders touching, on a bench deep within the park where no one was likely to come at midnight.

"I've been having second thoughts, though," he said. "I mean, no one in Darden knows about us. Maybe we should leave things the way they are."

But, someone in Darden *did* know about them.

The killer crouched behind a large ficus tree, peering at the two men through the areal roots that hung from the lower limbs and trunk. No more than ten feet away from them, he could hear everything they said, as if he sat next to them on the bench.

Dressed in a black nylon sweater with hood, black pants, and black boots, except for his pale face, he melted into the background. His eyes narrowed to slits as he watched and listened to them discuss moving to another state, one where gay marriage was legal, or maybe going there, getting married, and coming back to Darden to rub it in people's faces. The longer they talked, the angrier he got.

Finally, when his anger was at what he called his 'sweet spot,' that point when it hadn't yet caused him to lose control, but was still enough to motivate him, he reached down and picked up the big hunting bow and quiver that lay at his feet.

With care, he selected an arrow from the quiver, running his index finger over the tip, satisfied that the steel barb was sharp enough to do what he required. He then took out a second arrow, and after checking it, he clamped the shaft between his teeth. Not exactly the recommended way to do it, but it ensured the second arrow would be ready at hand.

He then laid the first arrow on the horizontally held bow and adjusted it so that the string was firmly seated in the notch at the end. Raising the bow, he pulled the string back until it touched his right cheek, sighting down the length of the arrow. He pulled in a lungful of air just as the skinny one leaned forward to kiss the other one, then slowly began to exhale. Just before he'd emptied his lungs, he straightened his fingers and felt a slight sting as the string snapped forward. Without taking his eyes off his target, he pulled the second arrow from his mouth, and within seconds was set up for the second shot.

The first arrow had found its target, the side of the skinny one's neck, and from the dark stream of blood spurting from around the shaft, the arrow had sliced through the jugular. The husky one sat transfixed, watching his lover bleed out in front of his eyes, blood covering his face and chest, his mouth opening and closing, but nothing coming out but little mewing sounds. By the time he realized what was happening, and that he was seeing an arrow sticking out of his friend's throat, the second arrow had already completed its journey, burying itself six inches deep into the center of his upper torso, piercing his heart. Death wasn't instantaneous, but he felt only the first burning pain before his body went into shock. Then, he collapsed forward. The two died together.

The killer put his bow down and stepped out of the shadows. From a sheath at his waist, he removed a knife with a ten-inch blade and stepped forward, whistling softly.

When he reached the two bodies, he stopped for a few moments and considered how he would arrange them. Then he decided that the way they were, in each other's arms, the head of the skinny one lolled back on the other's shoulder, was perfect. He only had to remove the arrows. Gripping the knife tightly, he set to work.

CHAPTER 16

Greg was just starting on his second cup of coffee when the phone rang. He put the Styrofoam cup down, careful to not spill any coffee on the case files on his desk, and picked the instrument up.

"Detective Kildare," he said.

"Greg, this is Marcus Stone. You and Larry better get over to Raleigh Park, stat. Stat, by the way, is a medical term meaning get your asses over here fast."

"What is it, doc?"

"More bodies, detective. Why the hell else would I be calling you."

Greg felt a cold sensation at the back of his neck. "Where in the park, doc?"

"You can't miss it. Just look for the morgue van and probably a patrol car."

Stone hung up. Meade was just coming back from the john. He had a satisfied look on his face until he saw the expression on Greg's face.

"Oh, shit, not another one?"

"Yeah," Greg said. "Raleigh Park. Doc. Stone's already there. He's the one who just called me."

The door banged open and Hoag, his face red, stormed in. "Greg, Larry, get your asses over to Raleigh Park. We've another two dead bodies."

Greg was standing and adjusting his service weapon. "Yeah, I know chief. Doc. Stone just called. Larry and I are on our way."

As they passed Hoag at the door, he grabbed Greg's shoulder, squeezing hard. "Greg, get this son of a bitch, and get him *soon*, you hear," he said in a hoarse voice. "The mayor's gonna have a coronary when he hears this. Holy shit, six murders in less than a week."

"We'll get him, chief," Greg said. "Tell the mayor not to worry."

Hoag, though, didn't hear him. He'd turned as he was talking, and was walking slump-shouldered back to his office, muttering to himself.

"You want me to drive this time?" Meade asked.

"Nah, I think I remember how to get there. Besides, I've got to learn my way around sometime. Let's roll."

Three of the town's ten squad cars were at the park, blue lights pulsing, and one was parked partially on the sidewalk. Greg shook his head. Dead bodies didn't justify such a response, but this was about the most action Darden's finest had seen, according to Meade, since the homecoming queen's float's brakes went out and it careened into the window of the bakery, taking out a week's worth of inventory and ruining the queen's tiara, gown, and expensive hairdo. Greg only hoped the officers weren't just standing around gawking.

Two uniforms were stringing up crime scene tape, and four others came loping out of the woods, heading for their cruisers.

"Where you guys going?" Greg asked.

The older one, a sergeant, stopped and frowned at Greg. "Figured you detectives would want to have any possible witnesses identified," he said. "Thought we'd cruise around and see if we can find some."

"Good idea. Thanks."

As they walked into the park, Meade leaned in. "You see the look on that guy's face? Bet that's the first time a detective ever thanked him for anything."

"Never hurts to be nice to people, partner. You should try it sometime."

"Hey, I'm always nice."

This new crime scene wasn't too far from the first one, so they didn't have to walk far. They came around a curve in the path and nearly bumped into Stone who, dressed in his white overalls, stood before a park bench, rubbing his chin.

"Whatcha got, doc?" Greg asked.

Stone turned and looked dolefully at him.

"A mess, that's what I got. Look at this."

He made a sweeping gesture. When Greg saw what was behind him, he involuntarily put his hand to his mouth. Beside him, Meade made a gulping sound.

"Holy shit, doc," Greg said. "What the hell happened here?"

Stone took a deep breath. "Hell, your guess at this point's as good as mine. It's gonna take a while to puzzle this one out."

You think/ was what Greg wanted to say as he gazed down at a scene from some drug-induced nightmare. Two men, young men, sat on the bench, and but for the bloody mess that was one's chest, and the mangled, bloody throat of the other, they could have been park visitors taking a quick nap after a stroll. Instead, he said, "What do you think, though, doc? Just a quick analysis."

"Well," Stone said. "The murder was done here. See the blood pooled under the bench. But, all that cutting, I think, was done post-mortem, or there would be a hell of a lot more blood. I think they were killed in some other way, and cut up afterwards."

Greg shook his head. He turned to Meade. "You thinking what I'm thinking?"

Meade shook himself and blinked. "Wha-? Oh, you mean whether or not this is the same perp as the first two cases? I dunno. Doc, is there a message carved or painted on these stiffs?"

"No, not on the bodies, but check the back of the bench."

They walked around, and there, in bloody smears, the words,

They which commit such things are worthy of death

"What the hell does that even mean?" Meade asked.

"I'm not a particularly religious man," Stone said. "But, there was something about it that triggered a memory, so I used my smartphone to look it up on Google™. It's a verse from the Bible, from *Romans 1:32* to be precise. The full verse is 'Who knowing the judgment of God, that they which commit such things are worthy of death, not only do the same, but have pleasure in them that do them.'" It's a verse about the hypocrisy of people who sit in judgment, but it's often one of the many that people use to condemn homosexuality."

"You saying these two guys are gay, doc?" Greg said. "How do you know that?"

"Because I know them. Gentlemen, meet John Willis and Colin Nelson. Ten years ago, they were the best duo on the football this town's ever seen. John was a quarterback who everyone thought would go pro, but he tore his ACL working out in the gym just before graduation, and Colin was his favorite wide receiver. Kid had hands like fly paper. A ball got anywhere near him, he'd snag it right out of the air. The two of them helped us win three consecutive conference championships during John's last three years in school." I know 'em because I patched up bruises and minor fractures many times when they were playing."

"Okay, doc, no surprise that you know 'em, hell, you know just about everyone in town. But, how the hell do you know they're, were, gay?"

"Oh, just about everyone knows that. They were even when they played football. They tried to be discrete about it, but this is a small town, and no one's business stays private for long. Of course, despite the religious and political proclivities around here, people chose to look the other way. Hell, these two were for a time the most famous people here, and no one was going to do anything to jeopardize that. After high school, well, habits die hard, and besides, they were both such nice boys. I don't know anyone in town who didn't like them. John was manager of the Winn-Dixie and Colin worked as a teller in the Mercantile Bank."

"Mercantile Bank? That's where our last two victims worked."

Stone nodded. "Yeah, but I don't think there's any connection. Neither Hal Burns nor Janet Croft moved in the same social circles as these two."

"Still, there are connections here, doc, that we have to explore."

"Enlighten me."

"The first two victims were students at the high school, the second two worked at Mercantile Bank, and now we have two more, who are alumni of the high school and one of them worked at the bank."

Stone laughed. "Sounds more like a jigsaw puzzle with the picture on the box erased than legitimate clues, Greg. I know you'll do what you have to do, but I think you're barking up a leafless tree with that line of inquiry."

Inside, Greg suspected—knew—he was right. "It's better than briefing Chief Hoag that we've probably got some religious nut running around killing people because he hears God's voice in his ear."

Stone's eyebrows wiggled and he pressed his lips together to keep from laughing. "I see your point. Well, once the photographer gets all his pinups and the techs have dusted for prints and other trace, I'll have the body moved to the lab. I'll get you autopsy reports as soon as I can."

Greg nodded in acknowledgment, and then he and Meade went about checking on the techs, who resented the detectives nosing in on their turf, organizing the uniforms who were still present in a perimeter search for clues—anything—that might help identify the assailant, and tossing ideas back and forth on how they were going to deal with what was rapidly becoming a small-town cop's worst nightmare.

CHAPTER 17

They spent several hours after leaving the crime scene interviewing the relatives and known associates of the two victims. In every case, those they interviewed had known the couple were gay and had chosen to ignore it until they decided to come out, and had no idea who would want to kill them. From the interviews, they went back to headquarters and briefed a worried-looking Hoag, who, for all his attempts to bully the idea of a serial killer out of everyone's consciousness, was beginning to suspect that a serial killer was precisely what his department was dealing with. For once, he didn't even remind Greg of the debt he'd incurred when Hoag had overruled the mayor and hired him. After the meeting with Hoag, they went back to the bull pen and updated the white board, typed up a preliminary report and added it to the file, and tossed around a few ideas—all useless.

It was after 6:00 pm when Greg finally walked into his empty house.

After taking off his gun and badge and putting them in the stand in the living room, he went into the kitchen. The first thing he did was take a can of Coors from the fridge, pop the tab, and drain half of it down his throat without stopping. After wiping his mouth with the back of his hand, he placed the can on the counter and checked the pantry to see what he had that could be put together quickly for supper. His choices were limited; pork and beans, spaghetti, or Korean ramen noodles. After a few seconds of cogitation, he grabbed a bag of the Korean noodles and a sauce pan. After putting water in the pan and putting it on the stove, he ripped open the noodles and dumped noodles, dried vegetables and whatever else it was the Koreans put in, and the spicy powder, and put a lid on the pan. He then stood there and sipped at his beer as the tangy aroma of the noodles began to fill the air.

After letting the noodles boil for three minutes, he poured them into a bowl, grabbed another beer and a fork, and went back to the living room. He flipped on the TV and tuned to a retro channel that featured shows from the 60s and 70s, just in time to catch an episode of *Sanford and Son* in the middle of an argument between the lead character played by Redd Foxx and his long-suffering son, played by Demond Wilson.

He almost sputtered noodles across the floor when Foxx, the irrepressible Fred G. Sanford, 'the G stands for gentleman', went into one of 'I'm comin' to join you, Elizabeth,' chest-grabbing pretend heart attack routines. By the time that show had finished, and *All in the Family*, with Carroll O'Conner as wannabe bigot Archie Bunker, started, he'd finished his noodles and the second beer, so while the opening song played, he went to the kitchen and grabbed two more cans.

He'd just settled back in his chair when the phone rang. He answered. It was Alison.

"I didn't interrupt anything, did I?" she asked.

Even if he'd been in the middle of an operation to remove his appendix, he would've said, "No, just sitting here drinking beer and watching mindless shows on TV."

"Good. I finished a preliminary profile on your unsub, and wanted to share it with you."

Greg had to concentrate to remember that the FBI used different jargon than local fuzz, and that an unsub was an unidentified suspect.

"Hey, that's great, shoot."

He could hear papers rustling in the background.

"Okay, the basics first," she said finally. "I think your unsub's a white male, probably in his late thirties to late forties. Sorry, I can't narrow it down more than that. This guy's either a doctor, had medical training, or served in one of the special operations branches of the military."

"Holy shit, Alison. You got all that from reading the police reports. And, how do you know he's not just a skilled butcher or farmer?"

"First; yes, I got all that from the reports and the photos. As for his profession, the wounds on the first two victims are too precise. This unsub killed both victims, in one case with a very precise slice to the throat that got both carotids, and there was no hesitation, and the girl was stabbed one time, right in the heart. Sure, a butcher knows how to cut a throat, but he wouldn't necessarily know where the best kill spots are on a human, unless you have a butcher whose customers are cannibals."

He chuckled. "Okay, I get your point, and I can see the doctor or medical training, but a special ops type or hunter, where'd that come from?"

"Well, the military trains these guys in close-in killing. And, the second victims were taken out with one shot each. No wasted rounds, and again, the slugs were aimed at areas of the body where a fatal shot is almost assured."

"So, a special ops guy who's also a hunter, I suppose?"

"Well, I'll admit, I just threw that in for fun." She laughed. "I wanted to see if you were paying attention."

"I see you haven't lost that warped sense of humor of yours."

"Nope. It's all I have to get me through the day anymore." There was a wistful tone in her voice that was clear even on the phone.

"Anyway, that's more to go on than we had. Thanks, Alison. I owe you a big one."

"I'm not done buster," she said. "The notes indicate this guy has some real emotional issues. You know what they signify, don't you?"

He cleared his throat a bit too loudly. "Uh, well, no as a matter of fact."

"They're rather inaccurate quotes of biblical verses referring to sexual misbehavior. In the first case, the two victims were unmarried, and in the second they were committing adultery."

Then, it hit him. The third case *was* related to the first two.

"Alison, I'm gonna tell you something, but first, you have to promise that it stays between the two of us."

"You have a third case."

It wasn't a question. He gasped.

"Damn, do you read minds?"

"No, sweets, but I read nonverbal signals, and the way you were sounding, it had to be the third case that would trigger bureau interest, and you don't want to officially involve the bureau. Am I right?"

"Only partly. I wanted to call the Washington or Baltimore field office on the first case, but my chief is one of those local cops who resents any outside involvement, and our mayor is even worse. They've forbidden me to even use the term serial killer."

"I told you, Greg, this guy's a spree killer, *not* technically a serial killer. He's not letting enough time go between kills."

"Makes no difference. In fact, if I tell 'em we got a spree killer, they'll really go ape shit, and my job's toast. The mayor doesn't like me anyway."

"That bad, huh? Why do you stay in a town where you're not wanted?"

"It's a long story, babe."

"Maybe I should arrange it so you'll have time to tell me."

"Huh?"

"Look, Greg," she said. "I'll respect your wishes and not file a report on this, but you guys are in over your heads."

"Tell me about it."

"So, here's what I propose. I have some vacation time coming. Why don't I put myself on annual leave and come up? I can consult from the background. This guy's gonna kill again; I can feel it in my bones, and you're gonna need help to put him away."

His head was spinning. Had he heard right?

"You want to come up here to Darden?"

"Sure, why not. It gets a bit boring here with nothing but students to talk to. I need to get back into the field again, even if it is sub rosa."

"But, once you check into a hotel, the chief's gonna know an FBI agent's in town. This place's small, and you'd be gossiped about within an hour of checking in."

"Well, why don't I not stay in a hotel?"

"Huh?

"Good grief, Greg. Has living in a small town robbed you of your verbal and reasoning skills? I can stay with you. If anyone asks, you can say I'm an old girlfriend, and we're considering getting back together. At least the first part's true."

He had to hold the phone away and take several deep breaths. He couldn't believe this was happening.

Finally, having gotten his breathing under control, although, he could feel his accelerated heart rate, he spoke, "Yeah, we could do that. I have a spare bedroom. But, aren't you worried that when you drive into town someone will spot you as a fed by your car."

"Oh, that's right, I had that big Chevy Suburban when we were . . . anyway, I'm driving a Prius now."

He laughed. "Well, that's different. No one will think you're a cop if you're driving a Prius. What color is it?"

"You won't laugh?"

"I'd never laugh at you, Alison."

"It's purple, well actually, violet."

He laughed.

"Dammit, Greg, you said you wouldn't laugh."

"I'm sorry. Purple? You're not kidding?"

"No, I am not kidding. It's a beautiful little car, and since I got it it's saved me a ton of money in gas bills."

"Well, hop in your little Prius and come on up."

"I'll be there tomorrow afternoon. I'll pack tonight, and put in my leave in the morning."

"You know I'm looking forward to seeing you."

"Yeah, me too. See you tomorrow." She made a kissing noise and broke the connection.

For several minutes, he sat there staring at the phone with a goofy smile on his face.

CHAPTER 18

He still had that 'walking on air' feeling the next morning, and even facing a white board that was covered in writing, but lacked even one single clue, his mood wasn't dampened. Meade, on the other hand, was a picture of gloom.

"What the hell are you looking so smugly happy about?" he asked Greg. "You get laid last night?"

Greg laughed. "No, nothing like that. I just decided that letting this situation get me down is not gonna help us solve these murders. I figured if I took a positive attitude, I might see something I missed the first time."

"Yeah, but whatever it is, we missed it the second, third, and fourth time as well."

"But, that's precisely what I mean. We went into things with an already negative attitude. I think that if we clear our minds and take a fresh look, things will look up. For instance, last night I figured out what the common thread is among our victims."

Meade perked up. He plopped into his chair and leaned forward.

"Yeah, what is it?"

"I guess you could call it sexual misbehavior," Greg said. "The first two victims were unmarried and having sex together, the second were cheating on their spouses, and the last two were gay."

"Last time I checked none of that was illegal."

"True, but to some people it's sinful."

Meade looked confused.

"It ties in to the messages left at the crime scenes, Larry," Greg said. "They're misquotes from the Bible about what is and is not permitted insofar as sex is concerned."

"I didn't know you were a Bible scholar, too," Meade said. "How'd you figure that out?"

Greg almost blurted out that he'd learned it from Alison, but caught the words just before they erupted from his mouth. "Uh, I got to thinking that maybe the messages might be important, so I Googled 'em, and bingo, I got all these entries with Bible verses. So, you see, I've already figured out that our perp's some kind of fundamentalist religious nut with a hang up about sex."

Meade pinched the end of his nose and screwed his eyes shut for a moment. When he opened his eyes, he smiled.

"Well, damn, partner, this emotional reset stuff of yours really works. I hadn't seen that connection before, but now that I hear you say it, I do seem to recall hearing something similar to the second message when my folks use to make me go to the Baptist church on Sundays."

"So, you agree with me?"

"It makes sense." He frowned again. "But, it still doesn't get us any closer to identifying our perp."

Greg considered his next words carefully. "One time, the department sent me to an FBI course on criminal profiling, and I still remember some of it. Now that we have a common thread, we can focus our efforts to finding someone who fits the profile. Of course, first I have to come up with a workable profile."

"Hell, that's all Greek to me, but if you can do it, and it catches this bastard, you and me will be the heroes of this damn town."

"Something to look forward to. Why don't you pull together all the interviews we did, looking for any indication of religious fanaticism, or even strong beliefs, from any of the people we talked to. I'll wrack my brain and see if I can remember enough of what I was taught to come up with a profile. Oh, one thing, ignore the women. I think our perp's a man."

"Why?"

"None of the three killings had the hallmarks of a female perp. A knife, a gun, and whatever the hell was used in the third case, it all sounds like some kind of macho, maybe even ex-military type to me."

"Around Darden, we got lots of macho, but I don't know if we have many ex-military."

"Run names through the database and see what pops. You might even want to contact the VA in Baltimore. They might know if there are any veterans living in this area."

With a specific task to occupy his time, Meade's gloominess was shoved into the background. While he got busy going through the files, Greg leaned back in his chair and thought about a way to introduce the rest of the information Alison had given him, and a way to effectively explain her presence when she showed up later that day.

The day passed quickly. They slipped out of headquarters for half an hour at mid-day for sandwiches at a nearby deli, and after returning pitched back into their respective tasks.

When Greg's cell phone rang, he glanced first at his watch before answering, and saw that it was approaching 5:00. He answered without looking at the number on the display.

"Hello," he said.

"Greg, it's Alison. I'm at the front desk."

"Holy-, hang on, I'll be right out."

"What's up?" Meade asked.

"A, uh, friend of mine's come to visit. She's at the desk. I'll be right back. No, check that, I'm gonna go home. It's already after end of shift."

He rushed out, leaving a puzzled-looking Meade gazing at the door he left swinging in his wake.

Alison, as beautiful as he remembered her, dressed in a light blue pants suit, her hair swept back on her head and held in place by two yellow flower pins, sat in one of the visitor's chairs in the public area. When she lifted her head and ran a slender hand through her hair, the breath whooshed from his lungs. He'd pictured her in his mind ever since the first call, but had forgotten how incredibly beautiful she looked, hardly the image one would have of an FBI field agent who specialized in profiling. She looked like a mature high school student. But, Greg knew better. He'd sparred with her a time or two at the Quantico gym, and even though he had a first-degree black belt in Korean taekwondo, she floored him two out of three every time they went to the mat.

She was as alert as ever, her uncanny ability to sense the presence of another person even when they thought they weren't making a sound. She rose and turned to face him when he was still six steps away.

The smile she wore made his heart flutter. When she fell into his arm, his face got hot, and he felt stirrings he hadn't felt in a long time.

"Greg, it's good to see you," she murmured against his chest. "It's been far too long."

The words he really wanted to say caught in his throat. He swallowed hard, and finally, said, "It's good to see you, too. God, you're looking so good."

"Ahem, so *this* is why you're not interested in any of the ladies here in Darden," Meade's voice said from behind Greg. "Can't say I blame you though."

Greg and Alison stepped back from each other, and Greg turned to find his partner standing five feet away with a mischievous grin on his face.

"Who is this?" Alison asked.

Greg cleared his throat. "Alison, this is my partner, Larry Meade. Larry, meet Alison Holloway."

Meade stepped forward, his hand extended.

"Alison, may I call you Alison, it's a pleasure to meet you. I didn't know Greg had such beautiful friends in DC. Makes me wonder why he left."

She took his hand firmly, shook it twice, and pulled her hand back.

"Actually, I live in Virginia," she said.

"Northern Virginia," Greg put in quickly. "We're old friends. Alison had a little vacation time, so I invited her to see the bay."

Meade bowed slightly. "Well, welcome to Darden, Alison: he said. "I'm sure you're gonna like it here. Say, what're you guys doin' tonight?"

"We're gonna—" Greg started, but Alison cut him off.

"I'm a bit tired from the long drive up," she said. "I think I'll just turn in early tonight. Perhaps another time."

"Sure. Raincheck, then."

Alison took Greg's hand and gentle tugged, motioning toward the door with her head.

"Okay, partner," Greg said. "See you in the morning."

As Alison and Greg headed for the exit, Meade stood in the middle of the waiting area, watching them with a knowing smile on his face.

Charles Ray

CHAPTER 19

Darden is a small town where everyone knows everyone else's business practically. The arrival of Greg Kildare, the hotshot former homicide detective from DC, to head the Darden police department's detective division was common knowledge.

The killer, though, was a bit surprised that a newcomer would be assigned to the six murders, much less put in charge. But, that was what the dolt of a police chief had done, which could present a problem.

Hoag and the rest of the Darden police force were known quantities. They would react in predictable ways, making it easy to elude them. But, this new man and his approach to a criminal investigation were unknowns.

He didn't like unknowns. He liked life to be predictable, because the predictable could be controlled. He did not like not being in control.

So, he had determined to learn all he could about Greg Kildare. In addition to an Internet search, which hadn't yielded much beyond some old news items relating to cases he'd worked when he was on the District of Columbia police force, he decided he would shadow the man, much as he would track an animal before moving for the kill. Get his measure. Determine just how much of a threat he posed.

Now, standing in the shadows of an elm tree across from the police department, he saw Kildare emerge in the company of a woman. Even from the distance, he could see that she was beautiful, and what was even more interesting, based on their body language, intimately involved with Kildare. Upon closer inspection, though, the hairs on his arm stood out, and he felt a tingle at the base of his skull. His lizard brain had kicked in, warning him that this woman was even more dangerous than Kildare.

She didn't look particularly threatening. Petite, attractive, if a bit subdued in her manner, she looked more like a mature high school student than an adult. And, she'd arrived in a purple Prius, which she'd parked at a meter near the police department, just the weird looking of vehicle the killer figured a teenager would drive. But, her body language with Kildare wasn't that of a teenager. It was that of a mature woman who had the hots for a man, but who was keeping her lust under control—just barely. For his part, Kildare was also physically attracted to her, but was holding back.

All this the killer got from observing their physical interplay as Kildare walked her to her car. He had no doubt they would throw off the restraints at some later point, and the thought caused his heartbeat to increase and his cheeks to turn red.

"Animals," he muttered. "Just like wild, rutting beasts."

CHAPTER 20

Greg and Alison stopped at a KFC on the way to his house and bought a family-sized chicken dinner with baked beans, cole slaw and mac and cheese. He explained to her that he'd forgotten to grocery shop and his pantry wasn't quite up to company, unless she liked ramen noodles and beer. She laughed and told him she would go the market the following day and stock his pantry.

Once they arrived at his house, he showed her to the bedroom, explaining that he would sleep on the sofa, and while she unpacked and took a quick shower, he put a bottle of white wine in an ice bucket and threw the chicken, beans and mac and cheese into the microwave to heat it up.

After Alison had showered and changed into an off-white Philadelphia Eagles tee shirt and blue shorts, she volunteered to set the food out while Greg showered and changed.

They ate in the living room, her looking to Greg quite fetching in the shorts and clingy tee, and him in a pair of cut-off jeans and a Dallas Cowboys tee.

"You know," he said. "We can never go outside dressed like this."

"Why? Are the people here some kind of religious nuts?"

"Nah. They're either Washington or Baltimore fans. And, I mean rabid fans. They make Chicago fans seem like slackers. I wore this to the market one day, and the damn clerk refused to check me out until I flashed my badge. He finally did, but man, was he surly about it."

She laughed. "Quantico and the surrounding area is like that, too, only they're only Washington fans. I went with some agents to a Washington-LA Rams game, and just to be contrary, I wore a Rams sweater. Well, those jackasses had bought tickets in a section of Redskin fans. Man, I stood out like a pimple on prom night in my Rams sweater, and when the Rams won it in the final quarter, and I cheered, you could've heard a pin drop around me. The temperature in that section of the stadium must've dropped ten degrees."

They both laughed at the absurdity of sports fans.

When the chicken was nothing but well-picked bones, all the sides and biscuits had been eaten, and the wine bottle was half empty, Alison turned to Greg sitting next to her on the sofa with a serious look on her face. "So, I assume you've told people here that I'm your ex-girlfriend or something?"

"Uh, well, actually I haven't told them anything."

"Your partner certainly seemed to think so."

They were both silent for a long time after that. She reached for the remote and turned the TV on. He'd left it on the retro channel, and an episode of 'Family Affairs' was playing. They settled back on the sofa, watching and laughing occasionally at the antics on the screen. Their bodies were close, but not quite touching.

He put his arm on the back of the sofa, smiling at the thought that his movement was reminiscent of times as a teenager when he'd take a girl to the movie and do just this to sneak his arm around her in the dark. He looked at her profile as she stared raptly at the flickering surface of his one indulgence, a big screen TV. His hand, almost of its own volition, moved toward a stray lock of hair that drooped over her ear. He smoothed it back into place. Her head turned, and he found himself staring into a pair of dark brown eyes, and felt a lump in his throat.

"I was stupid not to get in touch," he said. "I missed you so much," she said.

And then, they laughed at the way they'd spoken over each other.

"I'm sorry," he said. "I mean, talking over you like that."

"No," she said. "I'm the one who's sorry. We wasted so much time. I could've just gotten in my car and driven to DC. I knew where you lived."

"Or, I could've stopped being a macho asshole and called or driven down to Quantico."

"What stopped you?"

"It's a long story. I was tied up in this complicated case, my partner was killed, I went off the deep end. Hell, I don't know."

"So, why did you finally call? And, don't say it's because of this current case."

"It *was* because of this current case, well, sort of. I'm up against a brick wall, the chief, and the mayor on this one, and knew I needed help."

"Yeah, but you could've called Rick Meyer in the DC field office. If I recall, when you two were in training you were best buds. I'm pretty sure he would've helped you without running up the chain."

"I suppose so," he said. "But, when I realized that I needed help, you were the first person to come to mind."

"You ever think why that was? Why you thought of *me* and not Rick?"

"No, well, maybe. Actually, no."

She laughed and leaned her head into his shoulder.

"You want to know something strange?"

"What?"

"The day before you called, well, the night before, I dreamed about you, about us."

When she put her head on his shoulder, he abandoned all pretense and put his arm around her. Now, he reached over with his left hand and started playing with a lock of hair on the right side of her head.

"What was the dream about?" he asked.

He felt her squirm against his shoulder.

"Not telling," she said.

"That good, was it?"

He could feel the heat from her cheeks.

"Yes, oh yes, it was."

"You think maybe that dream was a portent of things to come?"

She pulled back and looked up at him.

"Is that your way of saying you don't want to sleep on the sofa tonight?"

He answered her by leaning forward and kissing her.

CHAPTER 21

When Greg left for work the next morning, Alison was still sleeping, curled into a fetal position with her hands clasped and tucked under her chin. He left a note on the bedside table letting her know he'd pick her up for lunch, kissed the top of her head, and left.

He was whistling as he walked out the front door to his car, unaware of the cold, unblinking eyes watching him through a pair of binoculars from the wooded area diagonally across from his house.

But, just before he opened the car door, he stopped and looked across the street. He saw nothing but the blank windows of a row of houses, and the thick trees that grew around and behind them. But, his neck itched, the same way it did just before his partner was killed. *Dammit. I thought all that was behind me.* Shaking himself, he got in and drove off.

The man with the binoculars lowered them and put them in the expensive leather case he had strapped over his shoulder. He didn't need binoculars for what he planned to do next.

Charles Ray

CHAPTER 22

Alison woke up to a warm band of sunlight shining on her cheek. She stretched lazily and turned over on her back, staring up at the ceiling, her thoughts drifting to the night before. A warm feeling spread over her body. It had been wonderful. She was glad Greg had invited her—or, rather, agreed with her suggestion that she come to Darden.

After a leisurely shower, she brushed at her tangled hair, and then rummaged through her still-unpacked suitcase for her gray sweat suit, the one without 'FBI Academy' stenciled on the front and back that she used when she wanted to jog off the marine base at Quantico and not be besieged by the FBI groupies who infested the area. She donned the sweat suit, a pair of thick white socks, and her battered old Adidas running shoes.

In the kitchen she looked through Greg's pantry, deciding that a shopping trip was definitely in order. All he had, besides a good supply of instant coffee and beer, were stacks and stacks of Korean, Thai, and Japanese instant noodles. She laughed as she stopped counting at forty, wondering how it was that he still had the trim body she remembered from his time at the academy.

Fortunately, there was a nearly-full loaf of bread and three eggs left in a blue cartoon in the fridge—she noted that he'd remembered her advice about keeping bread either frozen or refrigerated—so, she took a slice of bread, cut a two-inch circle out of the middle, put a pat of margarine from a crumpled package in the back of the top shelf of the fridge in a fry pan, and when it was shimmering, put the bread slice and the piece she'd cut out in, watching it sizzle for a moment before breaking an egg and dropping it in the cutout.

While the egg cooked, she heated a cup of water in the microwave, and dumped in a full teaspoon of instant coffee, watching the dark brown crystals foam for a microsecond before they dissolved, turning the water a nice mahogany color.

Greg wasn't good at food shopping, but she noted as she looked around the gleaming kitchen that he was still something of a clean freak. She'd noticed that in the bathroom, too. Unlike many men, he didn't have dirty clothes strewn all around, there were no yellow pee stains on the rim of the toilet, or clumps of little curly hairs in the sink from shaving. Even the mirror over the sink was free of streaks or stains.

Like many in her line of work, Alison was a multi-tasker. Often, when engaged in one activity, her mind was occupied with a completely different matter. That condition was operative on this particular morning. While her body went through the steps required to wash, dress, and prepare breakfast mechanically, her mind was busy on Greg's case.

Specifically, she was trying to get a handle on the personality type that would commit the particular killings that had occurred in the particular—well, actually, the diverse—ways that they had been committed.

The confusing thing was that each murder, or set of murders, had been committed in a different way; knife, firearm of some kind—probably a high-caliber rifle from the forensic reports—and some kind of cutting implement that the coroner hadn't yet been able to identify. If not for the biblical references left at each scene, it would've seemed that the murders were committed by different perpetrators, but she was sure they were all done by the same individual.

She was also sure the murderer was local. The circumscribed area in which the crimes had been committed, one of them being a spot known mainly to locals, convinced her that it was someone very familiar with the Darden area. What she couldn't determine was whether or not the killing ground was close to or far from the killer's residence.

The final factor that she'd been thinking about was the significance of the biblical quotes. They indicated to her that the killer had some real issues with sex, or what he viewed as sex that violated religious proscriptions. That, she felt, was usually the result of an overly religious upbringing. But, it left open the question of what triggered the killings at this particular point in time.

She had a picture in her head: white mail; over 25 probably, but under 65; fit, but not overtly muscular, a loner; comfortable with firearms; knowledgeable of human anatomy; completely amoral. In other words, she thought, smiling at the unscientific nature of her thought, a complete fruitcake, nutso, batshit crazy.

She whistled as she sipped at the coffee from the cup in her left hand, while with the right, she used a plastic spatula to flip the bread. The bottom was a nice golden brown, and the bottom of the egg was brown around the edges, just the way she liked it. She'd give it a minute to allow the top of the bread to brown, and the egg to achieve 'over medium' state, not so liquid that the yoke would run all over the plate, but liquid enough that she could use the circle she'd cut out of the bread to sop it up.

When she judged the egg was ready, she took a small plate from the cabinet over the sink and flipped the egg and Texas toast onto it. She then stood at the counter and began cutting the bread and egg into squares with the side of a fork.

As she ate, she thought more about the killer. Suddenly, as she bit down on a crunch piece of bread, an idea popped into her mind. She finished chewing, swallowed, and went in search of her cell phone.

CHAPTER 23

Greg and Meade sat astride their chairs, staring at the whiteboard as if willing the information they sought to magically appear on its surface.

Meade slapped his thighs and sat back on the chair.

"I'm getting nothing, how about you?"

Greg shook his head slowly.

"Nah, no matter how I go at it, I still come up with bupkis. We've got six stiffs, killed in two different locations, three different methods of killing. Add to that, these damn cryptic Bible messages, it tells me we got a loonie on the loose, he's probably a middle-age Caucasian male loner. That leaves us with probably a third of the men in the state of Maryland, and a huge percentage of Darden's population . . . present company excluded, of course."

"Hey, I only fit the age and race profile." Meade said. "I'm definitely not a loner, and I haven't read the Bible since I was . . ." He looked up at the ceiling. "Oh yeah, I've never read the Bible."

They laughed at his lame attempt at humor, but neither was feeling particularly happy.

"If we don't make some progress soon," Greg said. "The chief's gonna be on our asses."

"That's only because the mayor's on his. You know how it is; shit flows downhill."

"Yeah, I know. We're at the bottom of the hill."

"Say, apropos of nothing," Meade said. "That girlfriend of yours is a real keeper. I don't understand how you could leave her."

Greg almost said that Alison wasn't his girlfriend, but then remembered that was their cover. He also hesitated because, he had to admit at least to himself, he'd been thinking of the possibility of the pretense turning into the real thing, and if last night was a harbinger, there was a strong possibility. *Damn,* he mentally chided himself. *Got to get my mind back in the game. First order of business is to catch a killer.*

"We're thinking about our relationship," he said. "You know how it is with long distance relationships. You have to make sure they're worth the effort."

"You want my opinion? No matter, I'll give it anyway; she's definitely worth the effort."

"You could be right. Truth be told, I have been thinking . . ."

"Ah ha, getting serious, are we?"

"I . . . hey, let's get back to what we're getting paid to do. We've got a killer to catch."

Suddenly serious, Meade leaned on the back of the chair. "Yeah, I guess we should. So, what've we got to go on beside the generic, middle-aged white male with mommy issues?"

"Wha-, what mommy issues?"

"Sorry, couldn't resist that. I mean, with a religious and sexual hang up. Other than that, what do we know?"

"He knows the human anatomy, and he's pretty good with a variety of weapons, maybe ex-military."

"Or a hunter, like you know, a big game or professional hunter. Those guys sometimes butcher their kills in the field. They might know human anatomy."

Meade rubbed his chin.

"Yeah, but that's a stretch. Besides, in this town ain't nobody got the shekels to afford to be a big game hunter, besides old Maxie Caldecott the third."

The hint of a thought tried to announce itself in Greg's mind, but his phone rang, chasing it away. He saw that it was Alison's number, and his mood brightened.

"Hey, Alison," he said. "You're up. What do you want to do for lunch?"

"I'd like to try some of the local seafood," she said. "But, that's not why I called. I've been thinking about your unsub, and I had an idea while I was eating breakfast that I'd like to bounce off you."

"Sure, go ahead." Greg noticed that Meade was sitting looking up at the ceiling, pretending to not be listening.

"Well," Alison said. "What I said before still goes. This guy's a loner, not very social, but more than that, I think he views himself as superior to others, and has been appointed, or has appointed himself, the arbiter of their behavior. He's sort of like an ancient feudal lord who directs the lives of his serfs."

As Greg listened, that stray thought began to come back, what she was saying, along with what Meade had just said, was forming a picture in his mind.

"Well," Alison said. "What do you think? Does that help?"

"More than you know, babe." The word 'babe' had slipped off his tongue easily, and he realized that it was just what he wanted to say. "You just might've solved this thing. For that, you get a special lunch."

"I was thinking that I'd prefer a special after dinner dessert."

He felt warmth in his cheeks, and in lower regions of his body. "That too," he said. "See you at lunch. Around 12:15?"

"I'll be waiting. Love ya." He heard a little gasp, and realized that the words had slipped out of her unbidden.

"Love you too, babe," he said, and broke the connection.

He looked at Meade, an expression of triumph on his face.

"Okay," Meade said. "That has to be the strangest conversation I've ever heard one side of. Who is 'babe,' and how did she, and it better be a she, just solve this thing, whatever this thing is?"

"That, Larry, was Alison," Greg said. "I discussed the case with her last night, and she just told me something that tells me who our killer might be."

Meade looked skeptical, and a bit worried. "The chief ain't gonna be happy if he finds out you were discussing an ongoing murder investigation with a civilian."

"She's not . . . oh, never mind. The chief doesn't ever have to know, now does he? This is our case. We solve it, we're his golden boys."

Meade smiled. "True that. Okay, what'd your girlfriend come up with?"

"Our killer is not just a loner, he considers himself superior to others, standing above and in judgment of them. He doesn't avoid people because he's shy, but because he considers them inferior beings. You know anybody who fits that description?"

"Yeah, sounds just like that turd, Caldecott . . . whoa Nellie, you're not thinking . . . I mean, the guy owns half the town . . . we can't just go accusing . . . wait, he has that big collection of weapons. Holy shit!"

"Not only that," Greg said. "But, did you notice those pictures in his house. He's a big game hunter. He knows weapons, and I'll bet he's butchered a few in his time."

Suddenly, Meade's expression clouded.

"Greg, I saw something this morning. I didn't think much of it at the time, but now, I'm not so sure."

"What? What did you see?"

"Well, my commute takes me past your neighborhood, in fact it crosses the street you live on. This morning, when I was driving in, I saw Caldecott, all dressed in black, coming out of a stand of trees not far from your house. Like I said, I didn't think all that much of it. He holds the mortgages on half the houses in town, and owns probably a dozen. I figured he was just checking up on a tenant or something."

Greg's face clouded. "What time did you see him?"

"I don't remember exactly, but I was about five minutes behind you, so it would've been about five minutes or so after you left your house."

"Shit," Greg said. "I had this feeling I was being watched when I left this morning, but I put it down to PTSD." He noticed Meade's querulous look. "I'll tell you about it one day. Anyway, from Alison's description, Caldecott could be our man. I got a bad vibe off him when we went to his house, but put it down to my dislike of the filthy rich."

Understanding began to dawn in Meade's eyes. "And, that fucker's near your house with your girlfriend there alone."

Greg was already moving, adjusting his service weapon as he headed for the door. Meade was half a second behind him.

Charles Ray

CHAPTER 24

Her cheeks burning, Alison put the phone down on the kitchen counter and sat there staring at it.

"Did I just say, I love you?" she said to the countertop. "Yes, you ninny, you did. Well, did I mean it? Of course, you did, fool, and what's more important, he said it back."

Her lips turned up in the biggest smile that had been on her face in a long time. *He loves me.* Now, that would be something to tell her colleagues when she got back to Quantico. They would all be querying her about her trek to the boonies, and wanting to know what she'd done, and she would let them stew for a while, and then drop that bit of news on them.

She picked up her coffee, and sat back, sipping and smiling, not even caring that it had turned cold, and ordinarily, she hated cold instant coffee.

The ringing of her phone broke her out of her reverie. She recognized Greg's number.

"Hi, darling," she said. "Miss me already?"

"Alison," Greg said, tension in his voice. "Lock the doors and don't open them for anyone until I get thee."

"What the-! Greg, what's wrong?"

"I, we, know who the killer is, and he's in the neighborhood."

"Who is it?"

"You wouldn't know him, but we do. We interviewed him recently. Babe, did you bring your piece with you?"

"Yeah, it's in my suitcase."

145

"Get it. Larry and I will be there in ten minutes."

He broke the connection before she could say anything else. She knew Greg was not the type to panic. If he thought there was danger, well, there damn well was danger. She put the phone down and turned to go to the bedroom.

She was stopped in her tracks by the crash of glass and wood. Whirling, she saw a figure dressed in black, reach through the broken window frame of the kitchen door and turn the knob. Before she could react, he was inside the kitchen, no more than ten feet from her.

Despite her fear, or maybe inspired by it, she took in details as he advanced slowly across the floor. Medium height, white male, 35 to 45 years old, cold, emotionless eyes, fit but not muscular, dressed in black from head to toe. He carried an expensive pair of Bushnell binoculars in a custom leather case strapped over his shoulder, and a bone-handled knife with at least a nine-inch blade attached to his belt on the left side. He moved like someone with a lot of experience tracking game.

"So," she said. "You're the killer who's been terrorizing this town."

There was a flicker of surprise in those cold eyes, but only for a nanosecond.

"I looked you up, Ms. Holloway," he said, with the slightest trace of an English accent. "I see your reputation is not exaggerated."

CHAPTER 25

Her first instinct was to run and yell for help, but her training overrode what would have been a fatal mistake. As fast as she was, he looked faster, and at that particular time of morning there wasn't likely to be anyone who would hear her screams. If she ran, she would die.

So, she did the last thing he would've expected her to do. She turned square on him, put her hands on her hips, and smiled.

The flicker of his eyelids told her that movement had thrown him off stride.

"So," she said. "You know my name, but you have me at a disadvantage. I don't know yours."

"My name is not important. My mission is all that matters."

"Oh, is that so? What is your mission? No, let me guess. Your mission is to rid the world of sinners." She expressed it as a statement, not a question, to see how he would react.

His mouth opened and closed like a fish gulping for air, but only for a moment. This one was a cool customer. She wasn't what he expected, and he was confused, but was able to quickly get himself under control.

"You've read my messages? They didn't include them in the newspaper or TV reports. What? Did your boyfriend share them with you?"

"Yes, as a matter of fact, he did."

There, she thought, that hit home. *I wonder if it is was that Greg shared police information with me, or that I didn't correct him when he called Greg my boyfriend?*

There was a moment's anger in the cold eyes, but again, he quickly recovered. *This one's a control freak.* He smiled at her.

"I suppose I shouldn't be surprised that he would consult the FBI's top profiler. The locals would never have done that, but he's an outsider."

"My profile of you was incomplete, though," she said with as much calm as she could muster.

She'd been in the field on several occasions, and had even been involved in the takedown of a few perps, but never had she been face to face with someone she would unscientifically describe as 'pure evil.' Evil seemed to emanate from him in waves that threatened to overwhelm her resolve to remain calm.

"Tell me what you have, and maybe, just maybe I'll fill in the blanks."

Now, he seemed to be toying with her. *What's his game?*

"You seem to have a real hang up about sex, an almost puritanical view of what is or is not acceptable. Were you ever married?"

Sadness brushed across his face, mostly the eyes, that for the briefest of periods softened. Then, the hard, icy look came back.

"No. Next question."

Ah ha! A sore point. We'll have to get back to that.

"What was your relationship with your parents like?"

"Are you some kind of psychiatrist?" He laughed, a harsh, unfriendly sound. "You think I'm some kind of mental case? I assure you, I'm not."

"I studied psychology in college, yes," she said. "But, you're deflecting and not answering my question."

"You're a persistent one. I'm surprised that a macho cop type would be interested in someone like you."

He was exhibiting many of the traits of a sociopath, changing the subject, deflecting, anything to avoid directly answering her question, and worse, he seemed to be enjoying the little game he was playing.

"That's because, my profession aside, I'm a loveable person. Is that your problem, the important people in your life didn't love you?"

His eyes blazed with fury, for longer than any of the other emotions had. His lips quivered, and a muscle under his left eye twitched. He took a few deep breaths, and closed his eyes. When he opened them again, the coldness and control were back.

"I. Was. Loved," he said, speaking each word precisely and carefully. "I. Was. Loved."

"But, there were conditions, right? There are always conditions."

He blinked like his eyes had suddenly been hit with a bright light.

"What do you mean?"

"Most parents love their children unconditionally," she said. "But, some parents attach strings to their love, unrealistic expectations that tarnish the emotion of love for the one receiving it."

"Do you treat all your subjects to this crude form of psychoanalysis, Alison? Or, should I call you Agent Holloway?"

Alison eased backwards one small, slow step, watching his eyes intently, and hoping he hadn't noticed. Unfortunately, he had.

"I hope you're not thinking of trying to run away, Alison," he said. "I might not look like an athlete, but I'm in excellent shape. I've spent a lot of time in the bush. You wouldn't make it three steps before I'd be upon you."

"Are you former military?" she asked, more to keep him talking than anything else.

"Me, serve in the military? Not bloody likely. People of my station do not serve as common soldiers."

"So, you're wealthy. Why then do you find it necessary to kill people? Do you do it because it's fun, or a challenge?"

"It is not fun, and with these animals there is no challenge, none at all." His cheeks turned red, and his English accent became stronger. "I am merely ridding the world of sinners who deserve to die."

"Who taught you that philosophy, your mother or your father?"

At the mention of his parents, his eyes blazed.

"Do not sully the memory of my mother."

"You loved your mother, didn't you?" Her fear of what he intended to do, while strong, couldn't override her innate curiosity. He was a fascinating unsub, motivated by urges she was anxious to uncover.

"Yes, I loved her, and she loved me, but *he* was always coming between us."

"Your father? He resented that your mother favored you?"

"He did all he could to keep us apart, said we were dirty sinners. But, that's not so. Our love was pure."

The deeper meaning of his words hit her like a thunderbolt. She wasn't sure *he* even realized what he'd just said.

"He caught you two? What did he do?"

His eyes took on an unfocused, demented look.

"He beat me, and he locked her in her room. He forbade me from even being on the same floor. I was consigned to a small room in the basement. She died up there, alone. I wasn't even allowed to attend her funeral. Afterwards, he sent me to live with a friend of his in South Africa, where I was taught to hunt and track. I was only fifteen at the time, and I never set foot in this house again until he died."

"How long ago was that?"

"I don't remember. It seems like an eternity. Perhaps five years. What does it matter?"

"I'm curious to know what triggered you to do what you've done."

"When I first came back, I heard the rumors; my mother had escaped her room and run off. I hoped that she'd found happiness. Then, one of the older servants let it slip that she'd died, apparently of a broken heart. When I asked where she was buried, everyone feigned ignorance; said that my father had held a private ceremony to which no one else was invited." His eyes lost a little of their glacial quality, and shone brightly as if he wanted to cry. "I knew my so very aristocratic father would never be so common as to bury even a wife who'd betrayed him in a cemetery with the commoners of this town. I knew she *had* to be on the estate somewhere, so I began searching. It took me nearly five years, but I found her grave. It was, is, in a grove of trees on the bluff overlooking the bay. The bastard didn't even give her a headstone with her name on it, just a simple white marker. After I discovered it, I visited the town clerk's office, seeking her death certificate, and learned that he hadn't even reported her death. The fools in this town thought she was living in seclusion I the mansion, not venturing out, so they simply dismissed her from their minds."

"When did you learn this?"

"About ten days ago."

So, that was the trigger. Finding that the town thought his mother alive, but that his father had concealed her death. That's what drove him over the edge into insanity. "You know that what you're doing is wrong," she said.

"No, it is not wrong. The Bible says that fornicators and adulterers must die. I am simply carrying out what is required."

"You know, you still haven't told me your name. It hardly seems fair that you know so much about me, and I don't even know to whom I'm speaking."

He smiled. "I suppose it is only fair that you know. I, dear lady, am Maxmillian Caldecott the third. And, you are the first person in this dreary town who has the intelligence to even engage me in conversation. It is too bad, really, that I must now kill you."

He moved forward faster than she'd imagined he could, closing the distance between them in four strides, pulling the knife from its sheath as he did.

CHAPTER 26

As he moved forward, the point of the knife up, blade forward and a bit away from his body, she said a quick, silent prayer for the many hours Rho Tae-kun, the old martial arts teacher she'd met while attending the University of Maryland, had made her practice defense against weapons attacks. She'd studied taekwondo, the Korean martial art that emphasized use of hands and feet, for six years under Rho, gaining her third-degree black belt, until her FBI duties had restricted her to an hour or so a week practicing basic moves solo in the gym at Quantico.

Rho's words came to her, as if he were standing in the room: 'Keep body away from knife and stay in ready position. At same time, look for enemy weak spot, so when you stop knife, you can attack."

Caldecott was coming in low, and aiming for her solar plexus. A strike to the heart, and a clear indication that he was very familiar with the human anatomy. He was slightly to her left side, or his right, so she waited until the point of the blade was about six inches from her body and in a quick move that he wasn't expecting, she grabbed his right wrist with her left hand, pivoting right with her weight on her left foot. She then switched her weight to her right foot and grabbed his hand with her right hand, pulling her left foot back. It was all done so quickly, he barely had time to look surprised, when she pulled and twisted, pivoting left on both feet, and pulling him down toward the floor, using the force of his own forward momentum.

His head and body slammed against the uncarpeted floor of Greg's house with a satisfying thud, dazing him, and to make sure he stayed down, she released her right hand and making a fist, delivered six devastating blows, one to his forehead, two to his larynx, and three to his solar plexus. He made an 'oomph' sound when his head hit the floor, 'ungh,' when she hit his forehead, and 'urgh' when she hit his larynx the first time. For all the other blows, he was silent. The first two blows had knocked him unconscious, and part of her mind was aware of this, but her body was on automatic pilot.

She released her left hand and was beginning to straighten when the kitchen door crashed open. Whirling, she went into the ready stance, left foot forward, weight on the right foot, with her left hand up and the right between waist and solar plexus.

Greg and Meade stood there, out of breath, their service weapons out but pointing up at the ceiling, with looks of utter amazement on their faces.

She took two deep breaths and relaxed, letting her arms fall to her sides.

"Gentlemen," she said. "Permit me to introduce you to your murderer, Mr. Maxmillian Caldecott the third."

Meade looked at the unconscious man, the knife on the floor at his side, and whistled.

"Holy shit, Greg," he said. "You got to either marry this girl, or hire her for the department. She took that fucker down with her bare hands."

CHAPTER 27

Caldecott was out for an hour, time enough for Meade to cuff him, and for Greg to examine Alison to make sure she wasn't hurt. Except for a slight bruise on her right knuckle from hitting Caldecott's forehead, she was unharmed.

"Damn, babe," he said. "You could've been hurt, or worse. Why didn't you get the hell out of the house after I called?"

"I didn't have time. He broke the window and was inside before I could do anything. My weapon's in my suitcase, and he had that knife, so I couldn't call and let you know."

"Weapon? Did you say weapon?" Meade asked.

Alison looked at Greg.

"Uh, Larry, I have a confession to make," Greg said. "Alison's an FBI agent. She was my instructor when I took the profiler course."

"You mean she's not your girlfriend?" He smiled. "That means she's available." He leered at Alison.

Greg pulled her up and against his chest.

"Sorry, buddy, but that part of what I told you is true. I happen to have very strong feelings toward this lady, and I'll fight you for her."

Alison looked up at him.

"You're not kidding, right? You meant what you said on the phone."

He kissed her forehead. "Yeah, I did, even if you didn't."

She twisted around, grabbed his head in both hands, and said, "Of course I meant it, silly. It sort of just popped out, but that's how the brain works." She pulled his head down and their lips met.

"Okay, kids, get a room,": Meade said. "Shit, if it wasn't for bad luck, I'd have no luck at all. I finally meet a woman I can relate to, and my partner has already snagged her. Damn, you're an FBI agent, too. I mean, Hoag's gonna have a shit fit, but you solved the case *and* snagged the perp. I can't wait to see how he deals with this."

"Maybe we shouldn't tell him," Alison said. "Now that you've made it official that I'm your girlfriend, why don't we just go with that. Say he broke in, and you two got here in time to save the damsel in distress."

Meade jerked his thumb at Caldecott. "What about Sleeping Beauty there? What if he outs you when he wakes up. Plus, it could come out in his trial."

"Besides," Greg said. "I'm not comfortable deceiving my boss. I think I should come clean and tell him the whole story."

"You think he'll fire you?" Alison asked.

"He wouldn't dare," Meade said. "We just broke the biggest case this department has had in its entire existence. He might chew a few pounds off your ass for going behind his back, but fire you, no way."

"I've had my butt chewed before. I'm gonna tell him. Larry, call it in and have 'em send a patrol car to haul this piece shit to the lockup. I wonder how the mayor's gonna take all this?"

"Pruitt's a kiss-ass politician. When he sees how the people of Darden are happy that we got a killer off the streets, he'll find some way to claim some of the credit. Hell, he'll probably start telling people it was *him* that hired you and not Hoag."

Alison had been looking from one to the other as they talked. She laughed. "And, I thought DC was a political swamp. Looks like politicians are the same no matter where they are."

"Nah," Meade said. "In a small town, they're worse. You're closer to 'em, and what they do has a more direct effect on your life."

"So, why do you stay here?"

"It's home."

"What about you, Greg? Why do you stay?"

He looked at her and then at his partner.

"I guess it's my home now, too."

Charles Ray

CHAPTER 28

They radioed ahead that they were bringing in a prisoner, and when they arrived at police headquarters behind the squad car carrying Caldecott, Hoag was waiting for them at booking. When he saw who the prisoner was, he whirled on Greg and Meade with an apoplectic look on his face.

"Are you guys trying to pull some kind of practical joke? You do know who that is, don't you? And, why is his face all bruised?"

They both held their hands up to calm him, but his face was turning dark red, and he looked like he was about to burst a blood vessel, until Alison stepped up in front of him.

"That's my fault, Chief Hoag," she said. "The suspect broke into Detective Kildare's house, where I'm staying as a house guest. When I confronted him, he attacked me."

Hoag looked her up and down.

"If he attacked you, young lady, why are *you* not bruised?"

Alison smiled. "Because I have a third-degree black belt in taekwondo, and I work out religiously at least once a week—oh, and I don't think he knew that when he came at me with a knife."

Hoag swallowed hard.

"He . . . attacked you . . . with a knife?"

"Yes, right after he confessed to the six murders he recently committed." She stood there looking as innocent as a babe.

Hoag's mouth opened and closed several times, but nothing but a tiny dribble of spit came out. He looked at Greg.

You want to explain this, Greg?" he asked plaintively.

"Sure, chief. Larry, you want to make sure Mr. Caldecott gets properly booked. I'll go explain things to the chief."

Meade smiled. "Ordinarily I'd resent being assigned rookie duties, but in this case, I'm happy to do it." He started to follow the uniforms, then stopped and turned. "Good luck, partner."

"What was that all about, Greg?" Hoag asked.

"I'll explain it all in your office, chief. Oh, and I need to bring Alison along as well."

"Why is a civilian involved . . ." Then as his brain processed the conversation, he realized that Alison had said that she was Greg's house guest. He put two and two together, and for the first time in a great while got something approaching four. "Oh. Greg, you haven't introduced me to the young lady."

"Oh, gee, I'm sorry, where are my manners? Alison, this is Chief of Police David Hoag, my boss. Chief, this is Alison Holloway," He looked at her and smiled. "My girlfriend. She's vising from Quantico."

Hoag, beguiled by Alison's looks, was only partially listening to Greg as he stuck out his hand.

"It's a pleasure meeting you, Ms. Holloway," he said. "I was beginning to fear that Greg had no social life. Now, I see he left it back in . . . Quantico? I thought you worked in DC, Greg?"

"I did, chief, Quantico's only a hop, skip and a jump from downtown DC."

"Oh, yeah, that's right. I don't get down that way too often."

He ushered them into his office, giving Alison the best chair, leaving the wooden chair with uneven legs for Greg.

When they were seated, Greg looked at Alison, who smiled and nodded at him.

"Chief," he said. "I have a confession to make, but I hope when you hear it you'll understand why I did what I did, and see your way to forgive me." He then told Hoag everything, from his first phone call to Alison, ending with busting into his kitchen and seeing tiny little Alison beating the crap out of Caldecott.

When he'd finished, Hoag sat looking at him, his mouth open.

"Chief Hoag," Alison said. "I assure you, my presence here was unofficial and not sanctioned by the bureau. This bust is your department's, and you don't have to share it with anyone. In fact, Greg and Larry had come to the same conclusion I did that Caldecott was the unsub, er, perp, only before. Larry saw him in the neighborhood, and Greg called to warn me minutes before he came crashing into the house threatening to kill me."

"But, we'd never even have thought of him if we hadn't had Alison's profile," Greg said.

Hoag looked from Alison to Greg.

"I can't argue with results, I suppose, but what put you on to him, even with the profile?"

"A combination of things," Greg said. "He's a loner, but not for the usual reasons. He chooses to be alone because he fancies himself above the common people of this town. He's also a hunter, and he has an amazing collection of weapons, including knives."

"Okay, I can see that, I suppose. By the way, while you guys were out catching a killer, Mark Stone called. He finally figured out how the last two victims died. They were shot with steel-tipped arrows, and the shafts were dug out of their bodies with a sharp knife."

Greg looked at him, a knowing expression on his face. "Caldecott also has several hunting bows in his weapons collection."

"Oh, I'm not arguing that he's guilty. His attack on Ms. Holloway—"

"Please, chief, call me Alison," she said.

Hoag smiled at her.

"My pleasure, Alison. Call me Dave. Anyway, where was I. Oh yeah. His attack on you, Alison, clearly points to his guilt, but what provoked him to do that?"

"I think I hit too close to some uncomfortable truths for him."

"Such as?"

"His motive for the killings for one. He's a very complex man, and his family situation is even more so. He was motivated by a combination of guilt, remorse, and anger because his father caught him and his mother in a . . . compromising position, and punished the both of them for it, punished them severely."

Hoag looked confused. "Compromising position." Then, his face turned red. "You don't mean that Caldecott and his mother were—"

"Yes, Dave. A classic oedipal complex, complicated by the fact that his father then kept him separated from his mother until she died."

"Died? You sure about that. I've never seen a report of her death. Everyone thought she had just secluded herself at the mansion."

"No, she was locked in her room by her husband, and the son was sent to Africa, and didn't return to the U.S. until his father died and he inherited the mansion. He assumed at first that his mother had run away, but the servants eventually told him she'd died."

"And, all that caused him to kill people?"

Alison shook her head. "No, that maybe set the stage," she said. "But, it was discovering her grave on the estate, about ten days ago that was the trigger. The elder Caldecott had buried her in an isolated area of the grounds without even a carved gravestone to identify her. When Caldecott discovered that, he flew into a rage, and began killing sinners, most specifically sinners who violated the biblical restrictions on sexual activity. In a way, I think he was killing himself for what he and his mother did, which is probably one of the biggest sexual taboos there is."

Hoag sat quietly for a moment. Then, he said, "Greg's right, you know. We couldn't have solved this case without you. Greg, I owe you an apology. Your first instinct was right. I guess I've been listening to Dave Pruitt's bullshit too long. Can you forgive me?"

"Nothing to forgive, chief. If I'd been in your shoes, I probably would've done the same."

"As for you, young lady, this will be a real feather in you cap with your FBI superiors."

"I won't be telling them about my involvement in this, Dave. As far as the FBI's concerned, I'm on a vacation. I'd prefer to keep it that way."

Hoag looked at her. "You're not claiming even a tiny bit of credit for the FBI?"

"As far as the bureau is concerned, I'm on annual leave. In fact, when you brief the press, I'd really prefer you not mention my name."

Hoag smiled.

"And, you and Greg are really . . ."

She blushed.

"Yes, it seems we are, only it took him a long time to realize it."

Charles Ray

CHAPTER 29

Hoag honored Alison's request, and after briefing Mayor Pruitt, summoned the editor of the *Darden Gazette*, a TV crew and reporter from the local public access TV channel, and the stringers for the *Washington Post* and the *Baltimore Sun*, to the lobby of city hall and briefed them on the arrest of Maxmillian Caldecott for six murders. He gave full credit to Greg and Meade, stating that it was due to their innovative detective work and diligence that this case had been closed before even more people died.

The mayor, who had wanted his wife's cousin appointed to the position Greg held, and who, until that day had never once smiled at him, gave Greg a big bear hug and said the city administration would be treating him and Meade to a full-fledged heroes dinner and award, and how proud he was to have Greg as part of Darden's finest. Alison, who was in the audience, and who Greg had told of the mayor's attitude since his arrival, had to put a hand over her mouth to keep from laughing aloud.

Pruitt, all politician all the time, had, of course, to turn the press conference into an opportunity to make a political speech.

"Ladies and gentleman of the press," he said to the three bemused reporters. "The city of Darden takes the safety of its citizens seriously. That is why, after his brilliant service with the Metropolitan DC Police Department, we hired Detective Greg Kildare to head our detective division here in Darden.

Greg and Hoag shared a look. Hoag smiled weakly and shrugged.

Because they were behind him, Pruitt didn't see their byplay. He continued, "Detective Kildare, Greg, brings new ways of policing to our fair city, and I predict that this is just the first of many stellar achievements we will see from him in the coming years.

He paused and looked around as if the audience was much larger. Greg took a deep breath, hoping the man wouldn't launch into a campaign speech. Hoag looked at him and made a throat slashing motion.

"So, my friends, I would like to ask that we all give a great round of applause for Darden's finest, and for the finest of the finest, Detective Greg Kildare and Detective Larry Meade."

He turned, beaming his best 'get out the vote' smile at them and began clapping. The audience, apparently accustomed to Pruitt's impromptu speechmaking, joined him.

Hoag clapped Greg's back.

"Looks like you're one of us now, Greg," he said.

Meade jabbed him softly in the side.

"Way to go, partner. Told you we'd be golden if we solved this case."

Greg absently acknowledged their accolades. At that moment, all he wanted to do was get the hell out of the building and go home with Alison. They had a lot to talk about, among other things he had on his mind to occupy the day off Hoag had given him and Larry for closing the case.

Finally, just as Greg was on the verge of saying to hell with it all and walking away, Hoag stepped forward, gently inserting himself between the mayor and the microphone.

"Ladies and gentlemen," he said firmly. "That's all we have for now. His honor has important city business to attend to, and we of the police department have to get back to our mission of serving and protecting. Thanks for coming. If there are new developments, we'll get in touch."

Pruitt frowned, but Hoag put an arm around his shoulder and guided him toward the door. Unlike the press briefings Greg had witnessed when he worked in DC, this was not the loud free for all with people shouting and waving their hands. Here in Darden, with its press corps of seven weary looking journalists and camera technicians, when the police chief announced that the press conference was over, it was well and truly over. The camera crew started packing their gear, and the journalists started wandering toward the exit. Hoag managed to get the mayor into the elevator where he pushed the button for the third floor where the mayor had his office.

When the doors closed, he turned to Greg, Alison, and Meade.

"Whew, I'm glad that circus is over," he said. "Now, I guess you kids will want to get started on your day off."

"You got that right, chief," Meade said, heading for the door. "I'm gonna go change and head over to the café. Last time we were there, maybe it was me Yvette was looking at instead of you, Greg. I think I'll go find out."

They laughed as he walked away.

"You're gonna have to watch that boy," Hoag said. "He's a good detective, but he has zero impulse control when it comes to women."

"I'll do my best chief."

"Oh, and speaking of being a good detective, I know I've not said it much, but you're a pretty good one yourself. More important than that, you're good with people."

Greg tried to look embarrassed, which got a chuckle from Alison.

"Thanks, chief. I try."

"You do more than try, my boy, you succeed. Which is why I've decided to create a new position. I need a deputy chief, someone who can make sure all the personnel things get done right, but who can also supervise complicated cases."

Greg looked at him curiously. Darden's police force wasn't all *that* large, so he wondered where Hoag was going with this.

Alison, on the other hand, looked intently at Hoag, and smiled.

"I think that's a great idea, Dave," she said.

"Why would you want to add another layer of bureaucracy, chief?" Greg asked.

"Actually, it's not really another layer of bureaucracy. The person I have in mind for the job has a healthy disdain for bureaucratic restrictions, and is comfortable coloring outside the lines. Just the person to make sure we don't get bogged down in red tape."

It slowly dawned on Greg what Hoag was saying.

"Uh, chief, I don't know—"

"It'll be extra money in your paycheck," Hoag said. "I called the mayor before we came over, and he agreed. Plus, you'll get to work cases that you chose, since my deputy will be in charge of case assignment."

"Gosh, chief, I'm, wow, can I think about this for a day or two?"

"You've got a day off. Let that be one of the things occupying your mind." He looked at Alison and smiled. "Not the main thing, of course. I want your answer when you report for duty tomorrow morning."

Alison took his arm and squeezed. That was all he needed.

"You got it, chief. First thing in the morning."

Hoag watched them leave, arm in arm. He smiled like a proud father.

CHAPTER 30

Outside the city administration building, Greg and Alison stood on the sidewalk and gazed into each other's eyes. Both looked as if they wanted to say something, but was waiting for the other to speak first.

Finally, Alison said, "So, where do we go from here?"

"I've been thinking about that. You know, long distance relationships face a lot of obstacles."

She frowned. "Is that your way of saying you're not interested?"

Taking hold of her shoulders, he turned her so he could look directly down at her.

"No, babe, just the opposite," he said. "What I was about to say is, they face a lot of obstacles, but . . . the way I feel about you, I think we can handle it."

Her face lit up with a smile.

"Oh, well, I mean . . . I was sort of thinking the same thing."

His heart started thumping and he found it difficult to breathe.

"So, when you said you love me . . . you meant it?"

She tiptoed and kissed his chin.

"Of course, I did, silly. What about when you said it back?"

"Yeah, I meant it. I meant it like I've never meant anything before."

"Good. So, we'll try this long-distance relationship thing. What will we do if it becomes too much to deal with?"

He tapped the point of her nose with his index finger.

"Hey, you're supposed to be the positive one. If it starts to get tough, we'll deal with it, but, let's cross that bridge when we get to it."

"Just asking."

"You talk too much. I need to find something to occupy that brilliant mind of yours."

She leaned against him.

"Got any ideas?"

"Yeah."

"Well, are you gonna tell me, or what?"

"When we get home."

They headed for his car that was parked behind the building. Both had big, loopy smiles on their faces.

BOOKS BY THIS AUTHOR

The Adventures of Bass Reeves, Deputy U.S. Marshal

Fatal Encounter
The Marshal and the Madam
The Shaman's Curse
Renegade Roundup
Ma Barker's Boys
The Adventures of Bass Reeves, Deputy US Marshal
  (box set)
Bass and the Preacher

Daniel's Journey

Wagons West: Daniel's Journey
Wagons West: Trinity: Daniel's Journey, Volume 2
Wagons West – Bounty Hunter: Daniel's Journey, Volume 3

Al Pennyback mysteries

Color Me Dead
Memorial to the Dead
Deadline
Dead, White, and Blue
A Good Day to Die
The Day the Music Died
Die, Sinner
Deadly Intentions
Death by Design
Till Death Do Us Part
Deadly Dose
Dead Man's Cove
Dead Men Don't Answer
Deadly Paradise

Charles Ray

Kiss of Death
Death in White Satin
Death and Taxis
Deadbeat
A Deadly Wind Blows
Death Wish
Deadly Vendetta
A Time to Kill, A Time to Die
Dead Ringer
Death of Innocence
Dead Reckoning
Murder on the Menu
Over My Dead Body
Bad Girls Don't Die
A Deal to Die For

Ed Lazenby mysteries

Butterfly Effect
Coriolis Effect
The Cat in the Hatbox
Negative Side Effects
Murder is as Easy as ABC
Body of Evidence

Buffalo Soldier series

Buffalo Soldier: Trial by Fire
Buffalo Soldier: Homecoming
Buffalo Soldier: Incident at Cactus Junction
Buffalo Soldier: Peacekeepers
Buffalo Soldier: Renegade
Buffalo Soldier: Escort Duty
Buffalo Soldier: Battle at Dead Man's Gulch
Buffalo Soldier: Yosemite
Buffalo Soldier: Comanchero
Buffalo Soldier: Range War
Buffalo Soldier: Mob Justice

Buffalo Soldier: Chasing Ghosts
Buffalo Soldier: The Piano
Buffalo Soldier: Family Feud
Buffalo Soldier: The Lost Expedition

Other fiction

Angel on His Shoulder
She's No Angel
Child of the Flame
Pip's Revenge
Wallace in Underland
Further Adventures of Wallace in Underland
Dead Letter and Other Tales
The White Dragons
The Dragon's Lair
Dragon Slayer
The Last Gunfighters
The Culling
Frontier Justice: Bass Reeves, Deputy
    U.S. Marshal
Angel on His Shoulder-Revised Edition
Battle at the Galactic Junkyard
Mountain Man
Devil's Lake
Vixen
Awakening
Chase the Sun
The Lady's Last Song
Purgatory is the Next Stop
Catch Me if You Can

Nonfiction

Things I Learned from My Grandmother About
    Leadership and Life
Taking Charge: Effective Leadership for the

Charles Ray

Twenty-first Century
Grab the Brass ring
African Places: A Photographic Journey
  Through Zimbabwe and southern Africa
A Portrait of Africa
There's Always a Plan B
In the Line of Fire: American Diplomats in
  the Trenches
Advice for the Insecure Writer
Looking at Life Through My Lens
Ethical Dilemmas and the Practice of Diplomacy
Making America Grate Again
DC Street Art
Dead Letters and Other Tales: Revised edition
Things I Learned From my Grandmother about
  Leadership and Life, Second Edition
Feathers, Fur, and Flowers
Backyards and Byways

Children's books

The Yak and the Yeti
Samantha and the Bully
Molly Learns to Share
Where is Teddy?
Catie and Mister Hop-Hop
Tommy Learns to Count
Catie Goes to School

ABOUT THE AUTHOR

Charles Ray has been writing fiction since his teens. He won a Sunday school magazine writing contest when he was thirteen and having his byline on a short story published in a national publication forever hooked him on writing. During his time in the army (1962-1982) he often moonlighted as a newspaper or magazine journalist and was the editorial cartoonist for the Spring Lake (NC) News, a weekly newspaper, during the 1970s. In addition to his writing, he was an artist/cartoonist and photographer for a number of publications, including Ebony, Eagle and Swan, and Essence, and had a monthly cartoon feature and did several covers for Buffalo, a now-defunct magazine that was dedicated to showcasing the contributions of African-Americans to the country's military history.

After retiring from the army, he joined the U.S. Foreign Service, and served as a diplomat in posts in Asia and Africa until his retirement in 2012. He has worked and traveled throughout the world (Antarctica is the only continent he hasn't visited), and now, as a full-time writer, continues to globetrot looking for interesting things to write about, draw, or take pictures of.

A native of Texas, he now calls Maryland home. For more on his writing and other projects, check one of the following Web sites:

http://charlesaray.blogspot.com
http://charlieray45.wordpress.com
http://www.twitter.com/charlieray45
http://www.facebook.com/charlieray45

Charles Ray

http://www.flickr.com/photos/charlesray45/
http://www.viewbug.com/member/charlesray

You can also order some of my books through my author's website: http://charlesray-author.com/

Authors write to be read, and that can only happen when readers are made aware of the books available. Reviews are one way this happens. If you liked this book, please leave a review, even if only a few words, on Amazon or Goodreads.

www.ingramcontent.com/pod-product-compliance
Lightning Source LLC
Chambersburg PA
CBHW071718140626
46557CB00012B/946